THE MEMORIES OF THOMAS M'CLINTOCK

A QUIET WARRIOR FOR WOMEN'S RIGHTS AND THE ABOLITION OF SLAVERY

By

Richard B. Swegan

Mill City Press

Copyright © 2010 by Richard B. Swegan

Mill City Press, Inc.
212 3rd Avenue North, Suite 290
Minneapolis, MN 55401
612.455.2294
www.millcitypublishing.com
All rights reserved. No part of this publication may be reproduced, stored in a retrieval system, or transmitted, in any form or by any means, electronic, mechanical, photocopying, recording, or otherwise, without the prior written permission of the author.

ISBN - 978-1-936400-24-9
ISBN - 1-936400-24-3
LCCN - 2010933333

Cover Design & Typeset by Nate Meyers

Printed in the United States of America

To Mary Truman Welsh
My link to the past and our family's last Quaker

To Jennimarie D. Swegan
The joy of my life

Table of Contents

Preface ix
Historical Background xi
    The Schism of the Religious Society of Friends (Quakers) xi
    The Anti-Slavery Movement xii
    Women's Rights xiv
Principal Characters xvii
Introduction xxv
    January, 1870 xxv
    Philadelphia, 1890 xxviii
Chapter One: The Beginning 1
Chapter Two: Philadelphia 11
Chapter Three: Becoming a Member of the Society of Friends 23
    Establishing a Business 26
Chapter Four: Beginning a Family 31
    Marriage 31
    Family 36
Chapter Five: Public Life 43
Chapter Six: To Waterloo 63

Chapter Seven: Waterloo 71
    Photographs 88
Chapter Eight: Reform 91
Chapter Nine: Temperance 97
Chapter Ten: Anti-Slavery 103
Chapter Eleven: Matters of Faith 119
Chapter Twelve: The Women 123
Chapter Thirteen: Aftermath... 133
Chapter Fourteen: Changes Among Us 145
Chapter Fifteen: Home to Philadelphia 155
Epilogue 167
Selected Bibliography 171
Acknowledgments 181
Historical Locations/Web sites 185
About the Author 187

Preface

This book is a work of fiction, although Thomas M'Clintock was a real person, as are all of the other characters in this book. He was one of my great-great-great-grandfathers and, while unknown to many, he was a remarkable person who lived during a fascinating period (1792–1876) in American history.

Likewise, his daughter Elizabeth lived a dramatic life as an independent woman, an active participant in both the anti-slavery and early women's rights movement, and a Philadelphia businesswoman at a time when few women owned their own establishments.

While the events in this book are true, to my great regret Thomas did not leave behind any written memoirs. His memories and Elizabeth's comments are my creation of what they would have said within the circumstances.

Looking back from our twenty-first century perspective, we live in a world that rightly, in many cases, honors leaders who have made a difference in ridding our world of injustice and inhumanity. But it is often unsung foot soldiers of various causes who brought reform to life and fueled change. Among those who marched for civil rights, the men and women who served in our armed forces, and the silent army of abolitionists, countless men and women have stepped forward, often at risk of their lives, and truly paved the way toward a better future for us all.

My ancestors are such people. Their accomplishments and commitment to a wide range of reforms for the betterment of America humble me. I hope this book honors them in a way they would have found appropriate.

Historical Background

The years covered in this book, roughly 1800–1870, are probably best remembered by most Americans for the mayhem of the Civil War. But there was much more substance to the period. Countless historians and authors have written about the era from a wide variety of perspectives. It was a tumultuous time in our history. The United States was a young country, expanding rapidly into the West, dealing with complex political forces, and encountering new technologies. For those who want an excellent overview of much of this time span, I would recommend Daniel Walker Howe's *What Hath God Wrought: The Transformation of America, 1815–1848.*

The Memories of Thomas M'Clintock, while written as a personal memoir, covers the family's involvement in a variety of reform movements and historical events. In particular there are three major movements that the family was intimately involved in. These include:

The Schism of the Religious Society of Friends (Quakers)

While in hindsight the division of the Quakers seems like a relatively minor event, at the time it was traumatic. Particularly in Philadelphia, in the early nineteenth century the Quakers were a significant religious body and exerted wide influence on the community, business, and the politics of the day.

While their influence slowly diminished since the time of William Penn, they remained a force to be reckoned with. In present times, we tend to think of the Quakers as a small group known primarily for their peace testimony, but they were, at a minimum, a significant moral force in the nineteenth century as well. For example, they were the first religious body in the United States to take a stand against slavery and specifically banned their members from owning slaves.

Various authors have viewed the schism between the two factions of Quaker thought and worship from a number of perspectives: as part of the Second Great Awakening, as a conflict between rural and urban Quakers, as theological differences, and as a conflict between authority and power. Regardless of one's viewpoint, it was a dramatic event for the participants and caused a rift among the Quakers that took almost one hundred and fifty years to resolve. The Quakers divided into two groups, the Orthodox and the Hicksite, in roughly 1827 and it was not until the mid-twentieth century that the breech was healed.

Anyone who has switched religious faiths or participated in the division of a faith or church will recognize the emotions and anguish that goes with such an event.

The Anti-Slavery Movement

Prior to the Civil War and the resolution of the issue, slavery was *the* political, economic, and social cause of the day. Slavery was both a horrible ill and horribly divisive to the country. The question of whether or not slavery was moral or legal led to many arguments on the topic, and the question of the existence of slavery in the new states and territories dominated political discussions.

From our vantage point of one hundred and fifty years later, it is often difficult to discern why the issue was so contentious. Most, if not all, Americans now see the institution of slavery as an abomination. But that was not the case in the nineteenth century. The topic divided the North and South, split churches, led to violence and death, and was subject to numerous violations of fundamental rights protected under the Constitution. And that is just to point out some of the issues white America faced. For those held in bondage it was an unspeakable ill.

To empathize with the emotions and passion slavery generated, modern Americans should look to more recent causes such as the post-World War II civil rights movements, the Vietnam era anti-war movement, or more recently the conflict over abortion and gay marriage. Slavery was an extremely polarizing issue that likely dwarfed the more recent movements in the passion it incited.

Likewise, the common assumption among younger Americans seems to be that everyone opposed the peculiar institution. The truth of the matter is far different. Conventional wisdom seems to indicate that the South supported slavery and the North opposed it. While, with rare, brave exceptions, it is true that the South supported slavery, it is far from true that the North was unanimous in its opposition. The anti-slavery movement was certainly supported by the free black population and more obviously the slaves, but the number of whites who actively opposed slavery prior to the mid-1850s was quite small. While at its peak the white anti-slavery movement counted several hundred thousand participants, active white abolitionist consisted of a fraction of that number. And while many whites opposed slavery in principle, many were virulently racist in practice. To participate actively as an active abolitionist was to jeopardize one's livelihood, face opposition from friends and foe, and literally risk one's life for a cause.

The M'Clintocks were lifelong advocates for and supporters of William Lloyd Garrison's brand of abolitionism. Garrisonians believed in moral suasion as a means of eliminating slavery or, to put it another way, the power of their moral argument to compel others to forego slavery. The Garrison wing of the anti-slavery movement was often subjected to mobbing, threats of violence, heckling from audiences, and other forms of harassment. They were seen by many as threatening the very social fabric of the country, and to be a Garrisonian was to be always controversial.

Garrison, himself, served to generate much of that controversy as he took radical stances on a number of issues related to the abolition of slavery. For example, at various times he referred to the Constitution of the United States as a pro-slavery document—he's probably correct on this—and he advocated for the secession of the North from the United States and espoused non-violent resistance to social injustice. Wherever he could, he appeared to take the extreme position, which often brought more ridicule down on both his followers and himself.

Women's Rights

To talk about women's rights in the early nineteenth century is almost an oxymoron—for women essentially had no rights. Married women could not own property, divorce was incredibly rare, access to education was limited, access to higher education was non-existent, and women could not vote, to name a mere few of the legal limitations on women. While there are many reasons why this was the case, prior to the 1840s there was no organized movement to expand the rights of women.

There were certainly a number of influential authors and orators who addressed the topic, such as the Grimke sisters and Wollstonecraft, but there was little, if any, move to address those concerns in either congressional or state assemblies. One could safely argue that the abolition movement sired the women's rights movement in the US. It was difficult to argue that slavery violated fundamental rights without recognizing that the same logic applied to women. Women were extremely active in the abolition movement—organizing, conducting petition drives, raising funds, and conducting their own anti-slavery associations. Abolitionism in effect empowered women across the nation to both gain valuable experience and to realize that they were a political force themselves.

While the Women's Rights Convention of 1848 marked the birth of the women's rights movement with its list of grievances and the call for the vote for women, it was not met with universal approval. There was much resistance to the ideas of the convention and those who participated were subject to broad ridicule. The easiest way to measure the degree of approval the convention received is to note that it took an additional seventy-plus years after the convention for women to formally receive the right to vote.

Other events covered in this book may be unfamiliar to the reader, for high school US history books fail to touch on the many lives invested in these movements. A sample of such events include the life of John Brown, spiritualism, and the communitarian movement in the mid-1800s.

Brown was, to put it mildly, a radical abolitionist who believed in freeing the slaves through revolution and violence. While he is best known for his ill-fated raid on Harpers Ferry and his subsequent hanging, during his life he was also a source of controversy due to his actions in Kansas and the slaughter he led there. He remains a figure of much interpretation to this day; some see him as a madman and others view him as a martyr. The truth probably lies somewhere between the two extremes.

Investigation into the spirit world through séances, spirit rappings, and mesmerism was also in full force during this time. Growing from the Fox sisters, who resided in nearby Rochester,

New York, many dabbled in exploring the spirit world and found it a congenial movement. Many in the M'Clintocks' circle of associates participated in these activities on and off for a number of years.

Another movement that is referred to briefly is the communitarian movement. During the mid-1800s there were a variety of efforts to establish "perfect" communities. Some of these communities were based on religious beliefs, some on more radical premises such as "free love," but all shared a desire to create a more perfect society. Some groups such as the Shakers or the Amana community survive in one form or another to this day, but most have died out or left only physical remnants behind.

The M'Clintocks appear to have toyed with the idea of joining one of these communities and certainly provided financial support. George and Margaret Pryor did participate in one of those communities but it was not a good experience for them.

History is rich with passion as individuals pursued their visions of what the future could be, and the M'Clintock family was no exception to this, as the upcoming story will uncover.

Note: For those who may not be familiar with this era in American history, I have included a brief listing of the principal individuals, which can be found on the following pages. Likewise, although this is a work of fiction, the facts, events, and people involved in this story are as accurate as I can make them, and consequently I have provided a selected bibliography of sources in the back pages of the book.

Principal Characters

For reference purposes, I have included brief descriptions of some of the characters in this book who really existed. Many of these individuals are historical figures in their own right, and you can find additional information on most of them either online or at your library. Where a source or book exists that I am familiar with, and recommend, that is also noted.

Allen, Richard (1760–1831) was an African American who bought his way out of slavery. Allen became a minister in Philadelphia and is considered one of the Black Founding Fathers (with Absalom Jones and James Forten). He was the first bishop of the African Methodist Episcopal Church and minister of Bethel Church in Philadelphia.
　　See Richard Newman's *Freedom's Prophet* for an excellent discussion of Allen, his life, and influence.
Benezet, Anthony (1713–1784) was one of the early Quaker advocates for the abolition of slavery. Benezet had a strong influence on the Quakers' ban on slavery.
Bertram, Moses (Unknown) was a druggist in Philadelphia in the late 1700s.

Brown, John (1800–1859) was a radical abolitionist who believed in armed insurrection as a means to end slavery. He shows up at various points with the abolitionist movement and he had support from some of them. He is best known for his raid on Harpers Ferry and his subsequent hanging there.

Douglass, Frederick (1818–1895), a prominent name in history, was an escaped slave and one of the foremost orators in the anti-slavery cause. A powerful speaker, he was well known for his eloquence and oratorical skill. He published the *North Star* in Rochester and was an active reformer and advocate for the rights of African Americans throughout his life.

There are numerous works on Douglass, including three versions of his autobiography.

Forten, James (1746–1842) was a free black in Philadelphia and one of the richest men there. He operated a sail-making business that was extremely successful and employed both whites and blacks. Throughout his life, he supported numerous reform causes and heavily promoted self-help and education among blacks.

See Julie Winch's *A Gentleman of Color* for a thorough portrayal of Forten's life.

Garrison, William Lloyd (1805–1879) was the pre-eminent white abolitionist. He led the American Anti-Slavery Association in its efforts for years and was a passionate orator and editor of *The Liberator*.

Henry Mayer's *All on Fire* is probably the definitive biography of Garrison.

Grimke, Angelina (1805–1876) was the daughter of a slave owner. She and her sister moved to Philadelphia, became Quakers, and spoke widely on the evils of slavery. She married Theodore Weld, another reformer, and with her marriage largely withdrew from the movements of the day.

Grimke, Sarah (1792–1973) reflected much of the same life story as Angelina. She wrote *Letters on the Equality of the Sexes and the Condition of Woman* (1838), which was very influential among reformers. With Angelina's marriage, Sarah moved into the role of caregiver for the Welds family and lived with them for the remainder of her life.

See Mark Perry's *Lift Up Thy Voice: The Grimke Family's Journey from Slaveholders to Civil Rights Leaders.*

Hicks, Edward (1780–1849) was the cousin of Elias Hicks and a passionate reformer in his own right. As an artist, he is probably best known for his painting, "The Peaceable Kingdom," of which there are multiple versions referring at various times to Penn's treatment of the Indians and the Hicksite/Orthodox split.

Hicks, Elias (1748–1830) was a farmer and minister in the Society Friends based out of Long Island, New York. During his life he traveled extensively among Quakers on the east coast advocating his beliefs.

See Larry Ingles' *Quakers in Conflict* for a good description of Hicks, his beliefs, and the Hicksite/Orthodox schism.

Hutchinson Family Singers were a famous American singing group of the mid-nineteenth century. They were commercially successful and committed to reform causes as well, often singing at various reform and abolition meetings.

See Scott Gac's *Singing for Freedom: The Hutchinson Family Singers and the Nineteenth-Century Culture of Reform*

Hunt, Jane Master (1812–1889) was the wife of Richard Hunt and the organizer of the Seneca Falls (technically Waterloo, NY) tea party that led to the Women's Rights Convention of 1848.

Hunt, Richard (1795–1856) was one of the, if not *the*, wealthiest men in Waterloo, New York. He owned numerous properties in Waterloo as well as a woolen mill. While probably not an active Quaker, he aligned himself with many of the causes that the M'Clintocks supported.

Kelley, Abby (1811–1887) was a passionate reformer and speaker on abolition and women's rights. The M'Clintocks were very close to her and often accompanied her on her travels throughout New York. Kelley married Stephen S. Foster, also a reformer, and she is sometimes referred to as Abby Kelley Foster.

Lougen, Jermain (1813–1872) was a black minister based in Syracuse, New York. He was active in the Underground Railroad and opposed the fugitive slave laws of the 1850s. He also served as a bishop in the AME Church.

Lower, Abraham (Unknown) was a furniture maker in Philadelphia. He was active in the Hicksite/Orthodox split, and he held the reputation of being fairly hot-headed in discussions with the Orthodox.

Lundy, Benjamin (1789–1839) was an itinerant Quaker printer who was a passionate abolitionist. He published *The Genius of Universal Emancipation*, the first anti-slavery newspaper, sporadically through the years and was an early influence on Garrison, whom he employed for several years prior to Garrison's publication of *The Liberator*.

Lundy, Samuel (Unknown) was a druggist in Waterloo, New York.

May, Samuel (1797–1871) was a Unitarian minister and reformer, as well as a close associate with the M'Clintocks on abolition issues, progressive religion, and the Underground Railroad.

See May's book *Anti-Slavery Conflict,* originally published in 1869.

M'Clintock, Charles (1829–1910) was the son of Thomas and Mary Ann and was referred to by the family as Charlie. He spent his early career in business with his father, served in the Union Army during the Civil War, and after the war he moved with his family to Oil City, Pennsylvania.

M'Clintock, Elizabeth (1821–1896) was a daughter of Thomas and Mary Ann M'Clintock and an early women's rights advocate. Usually referred to by the family and friends as Lizzie, she was an intimate associate of Elizabeth Cady Stanton prior to her own marriage and subsequently moved to Syracuse and then Philadelphia where she established her own business and supported her parents in their old age.

M'Clintock, Mary Ann (1822–1880) was a daughter of Thomas and Mary Ann M'Clintock and the author's great-great-grandmother, variously referred to as Mary and Maggie in existing correspondence. She married James Truman in 1852. She and James were among the founders of Longwood Progressive Meeting in Delaware. Her reform activity appears to be minimal after her marriage as the mid-1850s approached. She died in Germany while James was attending the German court.

M'Clintock, Mary Ann Wilson (1800–1884) was the wife of Thomas M'Clintock. A committed reformer in her own right, most contemporary accounts place her as an equal, albeit less vocal, partner of Thomas.

M'Clintock, Samuel (1728–1806) was the father of Thomas M'Clintock Sr. and grandfather of Thomas M'Clintock.

M'Clintock, Sarah (1807–1842) was the niece of Thomas M'Clintock who married Richard Hunt. She and Hunt had three children.

M'Clintock, Thomas (1792–1876) is the principal subject of this book. His life is chronicled in the following pages.

Mott, James (1788–1868) was the husband of Lucretia Mott and appears to have been her partner in all things, but he took the quiet role of supporting her.

Mott, Lucretia (1793–1880) was a Quaker minister and prominent reformer, particularly with abolition and women's rights. She was one of the best known women of the nineteenth century and typically drew large crowds wherever she spoke.

There are numerous works on Mott including collections of her letters and sermons. Probably the most accessible book is Margaret Hope Bacon's *Valiant Friend.*

Mumford, Thomas (Unknown) was a Unitarian minister and editor. At the time of the Women's Rights Convention, he was editor of one of the local Seneca Falls newspapers. His obituary of Thomas is one of the contemporary accounts of Thomas and is often cited by historians when describing the family.

Parker, Theodore (1810–1860) was a Unitarian minister, transcendentalist, and author. Thomas M'Clintock believed his writing to be among the best on theological matters.

See Dean Grodzins' *American Heretic: Theodore Parker and Transcendentalism.*

Phillips, Burroughs (Unknown–1854) was an attorney by training and the husband of Elizabeth M'Clintock. He died tragically from a head injury suffered in a carriage accident. Elizabeth never remarried after his death.

Phillips, Saron (Unknown) was the minister of Wesleyan Methodist Church in Seneca Falls at the time of the Women's Rights Convention. He was the brother of Burroughs.

Post, Amy (1802–1889) was the wife of Isaac and a noted reformer in her own right. She was a long-time supporter and friend of Frederick Douglass.

Post, Isaac (1798–1872) was a druggist, reformer, and Quaker from Rochester, New York. The M'Clintocks shared many activities and beliefs including their interest in spiritualism, abolitionism, and women's rights with the Posts.

Pryor, Margaret Wilson (Unknown) was the half-sister of Mary Ann M'Clintock and was often referred to as Aunt Margaret by the family. She and her husband, George, lived in the Waterloo area and later moved to the Vineland, New Jersey, area. They were dedicated reformers but not very successful financially. Margaret served as chaperone to numerous women reformers, particularly Abby Kelley.

Purvis, Harriet Forten (1810–1875) was the daughter of James Forten and wife of Robert Purvis, the president of the Underground Railroad. Along with Lucretia Mott and Mary Ann M'Clintock, she was one of the founders of the Philadelphia Female Anti-Slavery Society.

Purvis, Robert (1810–1898) is often referred to as the father of the Underground Railroad. He was an active reformer in the Philadelphia area.

See Margaret Hope Bacon's *But One Race: The Life of Robert Purvis*.

Stanton, Elizabeth Cady (1815–1902) was the intellectual godmother of the women's rights movement and passionate crusader for women's rights and suffrage.

Stanton wrote a lot, and much has been written about her. See Lori Ginzberg's *Elizabeth Cady Stanton: An American Life*.

Truman, Catherine Master (1797–Unknown) was the wife of George Truman and descendant of members of the Pennsylvania Abolition Society. Her sister was Jane Master Hunt, who married Richard Hunt after the death of Sarah M'Clintock.

Truman, George (1798–1877) was one of the author's great-great-great-grandfathers. He had a varied career and became a physician late in life. He was a Hicksite, an active reformer, and one of the founders of Swarthmore College.

Truman, Howard (1866–1896) was the son of James Truman and Mary Ann Truman. Howard was a teacher and poet publishing the work *Echoes* shortly before his death.

Truman, James (1826–1915) was the son of George and Catherine Truman and husband of Mary Ann M'Clintock. A prominent dentist during his lifetime, he became head of the dental school at the University of Pennsylvania and had associations with the Imperial Court in Germany. While he was dean of the dental school, the first women were admitted to the school.

Wilson, John (Unknown) was the father of Mary Ann Wilson M'Clintock. He was a boat builder by trade and built one of the early steamboats (pre-Fulton). He fought in the Revolutionary War as a member of Delaware's Militia, and the family's oral history has him crossing the Delaware with Washington.

Woolman, John (1720–1772) was an early Quaker minister and advocate for abolition. He was extremely influential in getting the Quakers to abolish ownership of slaves.

See Thomas P. Slaughter's, *The Beautiful Soul of John Woolman, Apostle of Abolition.*

Wright, Martha Coffin (1806–1875) was the sister of Lucretia Mott and a long-time women's rights advocate. She was one of the few in the women's rights movement with a publicly displayed sense of humor.

See Sherry H. Penney and James D. Livingston's *A Very Dangerous Woman.*

Introduction

January, 1870
Vineland, New Jersey

I have walked with some of the giants of my age, men and women such as Lucretia Mott, William Lloyd Garrison, and Frederick Douglass. And now, as I near what must be the end of my days on this earth, I find myself reflecting on past events and occurrences that compose the purpose of my life.

This, then, is my testimony to those days and my buried comrades. It is my recollection, as best an old man can reconstruct, of events and time long gone by. Perhaps it is my vanity, but I wish there to be a record for my children and my children's children of the people, places, and events hidden in the recesses of my mind.

Like all such works, this is a collection of my memories and for that I am solely accountable. Various people who witnessed the events or heard the conversations may remember what occurred differently, and there may be as much truth in their accounts as mine. Only God and the conscience of men can decide in the end. I make no claim to be the source of all truth, as that resides with God alone.

May others read this as they see fit, and may blessings attend all those who partake of these words.

The pages that follow are organized according to my memory of the past. Much to my regret, as I write these words, I did not keep a regular journal through these many years, so as I delve into the past, any imperfections are based on my own failed remembrance.

My life has spanned dramatic days. As a child I have vague memories of the death of Washington, and I have lived through our recent tragic conflict to see new days approaching. Throughout the duration of my years, I have tried to live my life according to the dictates of God as I understood them. It has long been my belief that one's life is measured not so much in how one believes but by the manner with which one acts toward others. To that end I have tried to behave in an honorable manner, treating others as I would wish to be treated and acting against injustice, as I believed appropriate. Undoubtedly I have offended others as a result of my actions or works, and to those I have hurt I offer my deepest apologies for any pain I have caused.

For many years I have restrained myself, not wanting to speak ill of or inflict pain on another. Likewise, I have held myself in, suppressing doubts and fears. Only Mary Ann knows that which plagues my heart. I fear that inexpressive trait has led others to see me as pompous or sanctimonious. Here I will try to correct the record and let others into my thoughts and feelings, my doubts, fears, and opinions. I know there is risk in such an approach and I tremble lest my children or their heirs see me with feet of clay. But, above all I am human and frail. It is only just that they see all of me and come to their own conclusions.

I regret nothing that I did on behalf of the slaves or women, and I will stand in judgment of those actions. Of the friends I lost as a result of those actions, I have many regrets. While my actions by the light of day seem determined and resolute, many were the nights I spent in fear and prayer for the morrow. I would share those thoughts, those misgivings, and errors with those who follow behind me. May they judge me fairly.

Thomas M'Clintock

Philadelphia, 1890
From the Editor

My parents were Thomas and Mary Ann M'Clintock. Much of what I am is because of them and how I was reared by them. I loved them with great devotion, and I honor their memory.

Shortly before my father went to meet his Maker, he bequeathed to me, for posterity, his collection of memories. As my father gave me this untidy mass of papers, he asked for two things: that I hold it for his descendants, and that I not bring it to the light of day until all that are mentioned in his memories had gone to their reward. I deem that the day for that has arrived.

I have spent the last ten years reading and organizing his memories. As I have done so, and from the distance of years, it seemed to me that some events required further amplification. What my father assumed to be common knowledge has dimmed with the passing years. In the same vein, much of what he discusses I also observed. As a consequence, there are places in the manuscript where I have entered either my vantage point or provided what I hope is clarification for future generations.

To prevent confusion for the reader, I have noted where it is my comment and not the words of my father. All of my entries are separated by the symbol *** and begin with the notation EMP; for reading ease they are also in a different print to signify that the words are mine. Likewise, I have taken some editorial license with my father's manuscript. My father's speech was the plain speech of the Quakers and contained many uses of "thee" and "thou," which might confuse the modern reader. Being raised on the Bible and being a Quaker, his speech patterns and writing often sounded as if he was speaking in biblical times. As a consequence I have removed most of the references to "thee" and "thou" and simplified some of his language.

As well, my father references occasional dates in the manuscript that were important to him. On this I have changed the Quaker custom of the time which referenced the months by number, not their pagan names, to the more familiar calendar now in use. There are also numerous references to individuals who had the same name in the original manuscript which may be confusing for the reader. As a consequence I have made some changes in the interest of clarity. Both my mother and sister were named Mary Ann. When referring to my mother I have used Mary Ann. References to my sister apply Mary or Maggie. As well, by chance, there are numerous Elizabeths, all of whom were cordially referred to as Lizzie, including myself. I have used "Mrs." in some cases, such as Mrs. Stanton, to avoid confusion even though it was my father's practice to call everyone by their first name. In other cases I use the individual's full name to clearly indicate to whom he was referring.

My parents were part of the quiet, brilliant, and compassionate group that made a difference in our world. Their story—and indeed it is their story, although my father tells it—deserves to be told.

Looking back, while my father emphasizes his reform activities, it is also a love story. My father was hopelessly devoted to my mother, who was a power in her own right. While I do not believe I ever heard them utter terms of endearment to one another, it was evident to all that encountered them that they were a loving pair, each made stronger by the presence of the other.

Elizabeth M'Clintock Phillips

Chapter One
The Beginning

My life began in 1792 in Brandywine Hundred, north of Wilmington in the state of Delaware on the farm of my grandfather, Samuel M'Clintock. As was the custom of the time, I was born in my parent's house. The farm where my family resided was my home until my departure for Philadelphia shortly before the death of my father, and I lived there in comfort for the first eleven years of my life.

The farm, or plantation as my grandfather called it, was home to the entire M'Clintock family. Residing there, in addition to my mother, father, brothers, and sisters, were numerous aunts, uncles, and cousins, all engaged in the necessary labor for keeping the farm in order and reaping products for sustenance and sale. We raised corn, wheat, and tobacco as well as the animals used for milk and food. It was here that I learned to maintain plants and a garden, which stood me in good stead both for food and my chemical preparations when I became a druggist later in life.

For those who lived and worked on the property, it was a hard yet happy life. Days were filled with the constant chores and tasks required to maintain a farm, and our lives were governed by the rhythms of the seasons: plowing and planting in the spring, harvesting in the fall, alongside the long days clearing land, caring for the animals, and engaging in the seemingly never ending chores made necessary by such a life. We spent much time facing the whims of the weather and suffered occasional setbacks, but there was always sufficient food to eat. While we were by no means wealthy, the land provided the bounty we needed.

For a child it was a blessed life. While the other children and I had our chores and schooling, we were given free rein of the two-hundred-acre farm—both the fields and the forest. There were always places to go, new areas to explore, and my choice of peers with whom to share those adventures. While my memories of those days have faded with time and distance, I remember them fondly. I can clearly recall the excitement my brothers and I used to feel when we discovered arrowheads buried in the silt of the creek bed or other evidence of previous settlers on the land. We would spend hours pretending to be Indians living among the trees and creeks of the farm.

My parents, Thomas and Mary, were kind and loving, although stern when the occasion required it. Father spent his days working on the farm and Mother dealt with the house. Running the house in addition to watching over my brother, sisters, and me was a full-time endeavor, as we were full of the mischief that naturally accompanies childhood. I often wonder how Mother managed all that she did, for it seemed that she worked from dawn to dusk and yet always had time for one of the children if her attention was required.

It is said by those who knew us both that I resemble my father in appearance. While I cannot vouch for the accuracy of this comment, I take it as a compliment. I remember my father as a fair, sturdy man prior to his illness. My mother was a loving, gentle woman raised as a Quaker yet expelled from that group for marrying my father, a non-Quaker. As a child I deemed this to be quite harsh; admittedly I had little understanding of those events. While I gained greater understanding of this as an adult, I still consider it harsh and ill-

The Beginning

advised. Regardless, I have assumed all these years that theirs must have been a true love match for her to make such a sacrifice. From her I inherited the speech patterns of the Quakers and their approach to worship, although we did not practice the faith.

Both my father and grandfather fought on the side of the colonies during our war for freedom, and there were many stories shared from those days. In particular, my grandfather made much of having spoken to General Washington himself on one occasion as he led the army through the woods of Brandywine. While I was never told stories of battles or war, he did speak often of his encounter with Washington. Neither I nor anyone else on the farm ever tired of hearing my grandfather's stories, nor did he ever tire of recounting them in his thick Scotch-Irish accent.

To the end of his days, my grandfather recounted stories of the revolution and the rising for Bonnie Prince Charles in Scotland. While he was born and raised in Ireland prior to his journey to the colonies, my grandfather considered himself a man of Scotland. Aye, my grandfather was a wondrous storyteller, and I spent many a night at his knee hearing him tell tales of the old days or of his flight to the colonies. To his very end, Grandfather retained a hatred of the English, and he counted it as a major accomplishment to have participated in two uprisings against them. Only in my later years through the support of English Friends have my own feelings been tempered. Liberty and the right to own his own land was to him precious gifts. And it was through him that I believe some of those creeds were instilled in me.

His gift of stories was not a solemn affair, however. Grandfather maintained a keen insight and a strong perception of the humor in events and frequently evoked gales of laughter from the children. When he tired of telling tales of the past, and in indication that bedtime had approached, Grandfather would often serenade us with the playing of the pipes. He had learned to play as a young boy and continued playing throughout his days. We always knew whether he was happy or sad by the airs he produced for us. To this day I find the presence of music to evoke strong emotions in me as well—both for joy and sorrow.

My grandfather brought with him to America his Presbyterian faith, and it was in this faith that I spent the early years of my life aside from the example my mother provided. Church itself was a rare event, as the nearest Presbyterian church was some miles distant. My earliest memories are of being read Bible stories prior to bed by my mother or father. Those early evenings ingrained in me a lifelong love of reading and exploring the Scripture. It was from the Bible that I first learned to read myself. The study of the Bible is a habit I have retained throughout my life, to my eternal benefit. The Lord often works in mysterious ways, and I take great satisfaction in that fact.

As noted, my early days were filled with chores and play in the manner of children of that time. When I reached the age of four or five, my mother began the process of teaching me my letters and numbers, and it was from her that I began to haltingly make my way through the Good Book. My learning continued for some years at a school located two to three miles from our homestead. Each morning and evening during the winter months, my younger relations and I made the trek to and from the school through the woods. As was the case with my peers, I went to school, as all did, when the demands of the farm lessened and left my formal education behind when the seasons called.

During those schooling months, my brothers and I, and to a lesser extent my sisters, spent our daylight hours under the tutelage of several different teachers as it seemed that each year brought a new young man to our school. At the time I thought them ancient, although I now realize they were but young men. As I remember it, I spent the better portion of four or five years under the direction of these teachers, until I was older and left for Philadelphia. In total I suspect my formal schooling was limited to three or four years of education. During that time I learned to read and write reasonably well and to do sums, which my parents drilled into my malleable mind. I was also exposed to a smattering of learning in other fields, including geography, some philosophy, and a small amount of Latin. To my regret, I do not have a great gift for tongues and to this day require assistance in translating Latin, and particularly Greek, which has been a hindrance to me in my studies of the Bible.

While my education was brief by today's reckoning, it laid a foundation for exploration for the rest of my life. I benefited greatly by early on finding joy and illumination in the written word. Well do I remember walking to and from school with my nose in a book. Fortunately for me, my family was patient with me and protected me from falling or walking in puddles while reading. To this day, in my prayers at night I often give thanks to the benevolence of Mr. Spencer, the only teacher that I had for more than one year, and the care and inspiration he provided to me. I do not know where his travels took him, but he had and has at least one true disciple.

Education, learning, and pondering what one has deduced are the habits upon which one can build a just life. Combined with the blessings of God and the insight He provides, a person should be able to live a life of righteousness and truth acting in accordance with the dictates of God.

Before leaving my childhood behind, a few more words are in order on how we lived, as it was vastly different from today. Grandfather had settled on the plantation by about 1760, constructing first a rude log cabin, which was subsequently expanded into a clapboard house of modest size. Each of his male children followed the same pattern of establishing a house on the plantation and improving on it as they could over time.

The Memories of Thomas M'Clintock

The house my father and mother called home was very modest—what today might be called a cabin. It was no more than twenty by twenty feet at its largest and consisted of one open floor where we ate and where my mother and father slept, and a loft where my brother, sisters, and I slept after we outgrew the cradle. I do not remember much else about the house, although I have icy memories of how bitter the winters could be and how my siblings and I would cling to one another for warmth during the long, cold nights.

It was by no means a rich life in the material sense of the word. We struggled at times as all farming families do. Each illness brought the sense of death and too often it darkened our door. In the main, however, it was a well-spent time filled with love and exploration. Laughter served our needs when food did not.

For the most part, we lived a life apart from others, being primarily concerned with our own well-being and existence. We made rare trips into nearby towns to conduct the necessary barter and to purchase what supplies we could. These ventures into town, while infrequent, were occasions of great excitement as they were our only encounters with the strange outside world that existed beyond the plantation. It was, as I reflect back on it, an isolated life but one that was not wanting.

It is strange to me, in light of future events, that I made no note of slaves in the area, although they existed in Delaware at that time. I do remember seeing Negroes who were obviously slaves at the various markets we attended, but it had no impact on me. We owned no slaves nor believed it right to own another person, but slavery and the injustice of it did not personally affect our lives. I do remember that my grandfather could not continence the idea of one man owning another and would conduct no business with those who did. While I did not remark upon it at the time, as that was just the way we were and did not impose our view on others, I assume his stance had an influence on me and my subsequent views and activities.

The Beginning

My childhood and days of carefree freedom ended with the impending death of my father. Prior to his death from consumption, he had suffered from that dreaded disease for some years and was invalided for the last several years of his life. In his last years, God rest his soul, he was able to do very little, and much of my mother's effort went to his care and nurture. As I understand it, he passed away peacefully but suffered much on his journey to his reward.

Prior to his death, which he knew to be approaching, much thought and attention was given to the care of his children and my mother. As one of his brothers had removed himself to Philadelphia by this time, it was determined to seek his assistance in securing a situation for me. Together he and my mother's family, the Allens, were able to secure a position for me. As a consequence, in 1803 I was indentured as an apprentice to become a druggist under the care and direction of Moses Bertram, an apothecary in Philadelphia. I do not know how this decision was reached, but in the end it turned out to be a most congenial choice of trades for me. I bless the wisdom that went into this decision, although at the time I was terrified at the notion of leaving my family and the only life I had ever known.

In early 1803, during the height of winter, I and such meager belongings as I had at the time were placed in a wagon with my uncle to begin the journey to Philadelphia—a new world when contrasted with my humble origins. I can still taste the fear and grief I felt as I left my beloved family. It is an exceedingly perilous event to venture out into the world of strangers when one is eleven years old and sheltered from much that lies beyond. While I wrote often to my family and saw them on occasions over the years, I never saw my father alive again.

Through my years I have felt marked by this occasion and still hold its pain close. Perhaps this is why I still cherish family and friends and try to remain close to them and always in connection with them.

It is hard to sit in judgment of oneself as a child. Looking back on those distant days I suppose I was much like other children—full of the mischief, awash with curiosity, and yet fearful of the future, for I was all those things. I remember places and events more clearly than I remember myself and my thoughts. I can still feel the texture of things, smell the fresh scent of the plantation in the morning, and I can see the sweet face of my mother, but I remember little of myself. I cannot ascertain who I was at the time or see the connection of what I would become; all that is a mystery to me that I will never unravel.

I hope that I was an obedient child and one that my parents were satisfied with. While they never gave me reason to doubt this, they also never expressed it. While my parents were loving people in their deeds, there was little expression of that love in words or touch. This I hope I have corrected with my own children, for children are God's great gift.

I suspect I was seen as a serious child just as many see me as a serious adult. But, memories of my childhood are ones of friends, family, and laughter in loving surroundings.

***

EMP. Of my father's childhood, I know little other than what is contained in his memories. While we maintained relations with my father's relatives and saw them on occasion over the years, when he left for Philadelphia he seemed to leave his roots in Delaware behind. He did remark frequently about the pain his departure from his family caused him, and I do believe that it was a principle motivation for him to hold his family close for as long as possible. Indeed, when we children grew up and started out on our own, our moves caused him to follow us as if to hold the family together as one.

To this day, I still believe the hardest thing he ever faced in his life was Charlie's departure from the family when he chose to strike

The Beginning

out on his own for the western oil fields. The potential loss of close association with those who were dear to him seemed to cause him great distress.

I am also intrigued about his comments regarding his education, for I knew him as a learned man and a scholar. Growing up, the world of books was our constant companion. I can scarcely ever remember my father without a book in hand or, at least, one open to where he would eventually resume reading it. Indeed, some of my earliest memories are of my parents reading stories to my sisters and me. I know that he very much valued education and made sure that we all had the correct schooling regardless of our sex.

While a scholar and a man of books, he retained his love of the soil and land from his beginnings on a farm. I remember fondly his enjoyment in raising small crops and growing various gardens; he took much interest in horticulture and their medicinal properties. As young children we were frequently used as the subjects of various experiments that he would conduct on the effects of certain herbs or other plants when administered by mouth or in the form of teas. To my knowledge none of us were ever affected by these home remedies, but we were subjected to some vile tasting brews!

My father also maintained some of his grandfather's ability to tell stories with a twinkle in his eye, and he took much delight in tweaking the nose of the occasional English visitor with histories from his family and their resistance to the English. While not given to excessive humor, he did enjoy stories that poked harmless fun at the foibles of the human race.

While our pasts are so varied, my connection to my father far surpasses mere blood relation as I develop a deeper understanding of who this man truly was.

Chapter Two
Philadelphia

To Philadelphia

While the farm I was raised on was close to Philadelphia in miles, for me it was as if I was crossing an ocean to a new land. And in comparison to where I had spent my youth, it was an exceedingly strange land. The journey to Philadelphia took my uncle and me the better part of two days as we left the farm late in the afternoon of the first day. After stopping at a small rude inn along the way, we arrived in Philadelphia at midday on the second day.

I can still remember the sense of arrival in Philadelphia. Never had I seen so many people in one place bustling to and fro, always with a determined sense of purpose. As our carriage bumped along further into the heart of the city, we traveled down the broad vistas of Market Street passing by large brick building after building. During our sojourn through the city, my uncle pointed out places of interest from the time of Independence and the recent days when Philadelphia served as the nation's capitol.

I watched from my secure, small seat on the wagon, noting a range and number of people I could not have imagined. Sailors, Negroes, soberly dressed Quakers, well dressed men and women, and soldiers all crowded through the busy streets. Not only were there countless buildings, confusing streets, and multitudes of people, but the noise they collectively raised was most disconcerting. I felt at a loss and could not ever imagine how I would find my way through this vast city, let alone survive in it.

My uncle had informed me that we would spend my first night in Philadelphia in his home, and on the morrow I would be delivered to my master to commence my duties. Even secure in the bosom of my aunt, uncle, and cousins, I spent a restless, fearful night unsure as to what I would encounter on the morrow. Many are the nights I have lain awake and fretted about what the morrow might bring. Until this time I do not remember having those fears, but they have stayed with me at various points throughout the rest of my life.

Early the next day I said my good-byes to my uncle's family and departed to my new lodging and employer. I have little recollection of the first days at my new establishment, although I was strangely disoriented and confused for some time. I do remember being shown to where I would sleep, what my duties would entail, and little more. Being left to my own devices with strangers who controlled my life was most vexing.

Fortunately for me, my life soon entered into a routine from which I could make some sense and order. As the newest of the few apprentices at Moses Bertram's store, my duties were simple. I was to rise before the opening of the store and, if needed, tend first to the fire to provide warmth for the apothecary. Then I was to sweep the floors, dust the glass, and otherwise clean and straighten the establishment. Beyond that I was to act as the delivery boy carrying medicines to customers throughout the city and on occasion assisting matrons and servants with parcels and packages. It was in this manner that I learned my way around the city—making careful note of landmarks, turns, and buildings so that I should not become lost. In short time I became comfortable with the city of Brotherly Love and would spend my errand time taking in the sights of that grand metropolis as opposed to watching furtively, lest I become lost and confused.

Beyond those initial duties I had very little to do other than to observe the goings on of the store and Moses Bertram, although even that task seemed impossible. The store was lined on both sides with numerous tall shelves. Each shelf or case contained bottles of salves, ointments, or potions. As I later learned, one side of the store was reserved for those compounds that came pre-mixed and prepared by other chemists or doctors. Bertram often ran broadsheets advertising these potions in the local newspapers, and customers would come in to purchase these remedies for various afflictions, often with the assistance of Moses Bertram and later, as I became more knowledgeable, with my assistance as well. During these days the line between a physician and druggist were somewhat vague, and we often offered advice for the treatment of various illnesses that might now be brought to the attention of a physician.

The other side of the store, where Bertram spent most of his time, consisted of a vast array of bottles and containers containing various chemicals, herbs, and remedies, all of which required the preparation and attention that only he could provide. Usually these chemicals were to be combined into compounds, salves, or tablets. As my duties progressed in the store, I gradually learned the properties of the various chemicals, their uses, and how they could be combined into helpful elixirs.

This side of the store, really the domain of the chemist, was completely befuddling at first. Even though each bottle or vial was neatly labeled, I had no knowledge of what the label meant or the purpose or properties of the contents. In addition to the array of chemicals of which I had no knowledge, the machinations and thoughts of Bertram in combining chemicals was an even greater mystery, seemingly shrouded in arcane lore and knowledge.

Over time I learned, but it was a slow process. With every day that passed, I added a small artifact to my store of knowledge as a fledgling chemist. Whether it was the properties of a certain salve, or the types of questions (and which were appropriate) to ask a matron to suggest the proper treatment, each day added something to my understanding.

As my knowledge of the store's offerings grew, so did my grasp of the world around me. Not only did we receive questions as to the treatment of the various illnesses of the day (consumption and yellow fever being the most common), so also did we encounter questions regarding social ills and their effects, as well as what might be called "family questions" of a more private nature. Indeed every item regarding a person or family's health and lives seemed to pass through our doors—some as simple as dealing with headaches or pains and others as frustrating as how to comfort and provide ease to the dying. In short, all the good and evil of human nature trod into the shop in one form or another. Of course, as a young apprentice and young man, I was not exposed to much of this at first, but over the course of days and years I became trusted.

I learned much by asking. Often Moses, for that is what I learned to call him, would engage in private consultations with customers that I was not privy to. I soon learned that Moses welcomed my curiosity, and he always had time at the end of a day or during lulls at the store to answer my ready list of questions. I learned much more from him than how to become a good chemist, for he always took the time to listen to my inquiries and to respond with patience and kindness. Further, he allowed me to experiment with my own recipes and his in order to further my education. Many of the recipes I use today I either borrowed from Moses or developed on my own during this time.

In my youthful fear I took great comfort in his reassurance and calm good nature. He taught me lessons in life that I would not find

Philadelphia

in books, and I treasure his kind words. I have tried through the years to use his methods as guidance for me in my encounters with others and my own children. He was always fair, courteous, and pleasant with others regardless of the station of life occupied by those that he encountered, for he treated all as he treated me.

While I was not aware of it at the time, I now realize that Moses taught me not only about chemicals, their preparation, and healing properties, but also how to run a commercial establishment. He allowed me insight into how to negotiate with those that supplied him, how to set fair prices for products, and the countless other tasks beyond mixing chemicals that were necessary for a successful business. He has long gone to meet his Maker, but there is not a day that goes by that I do not engage in some task that I initially learned to do from him.

As I learned more about becoming a chemist, so I learned more about myself and the world around me. While my duties at the store seemed endless and constant—beginning before the store opened and continuing for at least an hour after closing in the evening—Moses made no demands on my time beyond that which was necessary for the successful operation of the store. As a consequence, I did have some limited time to engage in other pursuits, primarily in the evening and on the Sabbath.

***

EMP. My father was an exceedingly modest man. In all my years under his wing, I do not believe I ever heard him utter a word in praise of himself—rather, he'd usually deflect any praise for accomplishments to others. But he was, I believe, a superb chemist. On this I can speak from direct experience.

During our years in Waterloo, I often worked alongside him in the store. Not only was he able to mold me into a competent chemist (an area in which I had little natural talent or inclination), but

I had the opportunity to see and hear the comments from various doctors, read the letters from other chemists requesting assistance, and hear the satisfaction many of his customers had with his mixtures and potions. He and Isaac Post frequently exchanged recipes and maintained a vigorous correspondence over assorted issues and dilemmas they faced as druggists. At various times, he also took some of his recipes to market with the hope that they would find broader appeal, but he was not inclined to vigorously pursue this, and most of the appeal of his preparations and salves languished beyond Waterloo and Seneca Falls..

Likewise, I think he learned Mr. Bertram's lessons well. He took time with others, listened to them intently, and treated all with great kindness and gentleness. This was not always easy to do, particularly in the early years in Waterloo, but he was nothing if not persistent.

It was as a person of commerce that I probably learned the most from him and obtained my own desire to establish my own way in the world of trade. As my father saw that I did not have much inclination as a chemist, he did turn over to me other aspects of the business. I maintained correspondence, ensured that bills were paid, ordered supplies, and maintained the ledger of the store. He also allowed me to run small parts of the store, such as the books section, as my own, and this, too, turned out to be an invaluable experience and preparation for later life. All of this was crucial when I struck out on my own.

In all this he provided continual support, ever listening to my dreams, and never indicating that they were impossible to achieve. This was both who he was and an indication of his application of the lessons he had learned from Moses Bertram. I did have my own resentments at times as he seemed to defer to Charles on establishing a business but, in the end, he was a source of great support to me, in all ways, when I established my own shop. Just as he embraced lessons from his mentors, so I valued the lessons Father taught me, holding fast to them as I grew older.

***

Two personal pursuits filled the few hours of free time amid my daily busyness. The first and most important to me was reading and study. As was my custom, I had continued to read the Bible each evening before retiring. Moses, who had made note of this and who was himself a self-taught man, subsequently encouraged me to expand my horizons by engaging in a course of self-study and learning.

Being in the city of Franklin, it was expected that each man would work to improve himself for the betterment of all. Indeed, that beloved man went so far as to give me some hours off each week in which I might avail myself of the free library in Philadelphia. This was a gift from which I have reaped continual blessings. There, in the library, I was exposed to and had access to the sum knowledge and experience of mankind. I honored this gift by reading as much as I could across a range of disciplines.

I confess that at first I felt like something of an ignorant and naïve visitor from the farm. Many people who came into the store discussed books or events that I was completely unknowing about, and I found this to be an embarrassment. To this day I cannot abide being caught unaware on matters of intellect or learning. Having the time to read and reflect was a boon and comfort to me. It is a habit that has sustained me to the present.

While I read widely, trying to make up for a missed education, I found myself drawn most frequently to religious tracts, commentary on the Bible, and other works of a religious or philosophical nature. While in my later years I read the works of Dickens, Hawthorne, Stowe, and others of that ilk, I continue to gravitate to the thoughts of others on religion and similar topics. I did, I confess, read the occasional poet who seemed to express emotions that I could not contain, and indeed dabbled in my own doggerel at points of my youth, yet it was but a passing fancy. I soon found that I had no talent with poetry or ease of rhyme, but I have maintained an interest in reading poets of various genres throughout my life.

My habit, which began then and continues to this day whenever possible, was to read in the hour before bed and then to engage in whatever correspondence and letters were waiting. On those occasions where the demand of response did not beckon to me, I spent the time before sleep in reflection on what I had been reading or other issues that pressed upon my mind. This practice has been with me throughout my life. Indeed, I take note of the fact that the first book I ever purchased with my own funds, beyond the Bible, was a dictionary, for I found that volume crucial to my study of all other books. I took joy in learning new words and increasing my understanding of the writing of others.

***

EMP. As his own words attest, my father loved books. Simply holding one was a pleasure to him, even when he disagreed with the author's sentiments. We were not a wealthy family by any means, but my father always had funds for the purchase of books and took much pride in his small library. To my knowledge he never parted with a book he had purchased, and until the end of his days he kept his much beloved and much tattered dictionary that was his first purchase. We could skimp on other matters, but reading and books always took precedence over other expenditures.

***

The other pursuit which stole my interest during this time of my apprenticeship was to begin to make the acquaintance of other young boys who shared my circumstances or whose path I did cross.

Philadelphia

Over time I formed friendships with four or five other young men who either lived nearby or were themselves apprentices to nearby merchants. My friends and I did the things that were common to boys of my era. We roamed the city, particularly the harbor, seeing the sights and gaining new experiences. While we enjoyed mischief and good humor, in looking back, we were never a nuisance or rude to others, which I count as both a combination of good fortune and good virtue. Likewise, I count it a blessing that we were never exposed to or lured by the perils of drink or the other more worldly evils, which existed in abundance. We certainly saw those evils, but through the grace of God we were not tempted to indulge in them. I know not whether that was a result of good upbringing or simply good luck.

Chief among my friends were two who have remained dear to me for more than fifty years now. The first of these was George Truman, the son of Quakers who traced their heritage to the days of William Penn in Philadelphia. George was intelligent and well mannered but full of mischief as a lad. He, most of all, made the suggestions for adventures that would have appalled his parents if they had known. Most often these adventures involved forays to the harbor to see the comings and goings of ships, cargos, and crews, as George fancied that he would one day like to set sail and explore the world. Brave sentiments for the son of a sober, conservative Quaker family. I number his lasting friendship as one of the joys of my life. It has always seemed fitting to me that our families would one day be joined through the bonds of matrimony and become as one.

Another intimate friend was Abraham Lower, also a Quaker, who at the time was apprenticed to become a cabinet maker. Abraham was quite the opposite of George in temperament, as he was often hotheaded and sometimes spoke without regard to the consequences. But he never meant ill of it or directed comments to others that would injure them. It was simply his nature to speak that which he felt, which on occasion could be seen as rash or foolish.

All was not adventure with my closest companions. We also shared with one another what we had been reading, often reading aloud to each other and discoursing on the merits of the various thoughts we heard expressed by others. In this manner I continued my education and first learned to express myself in ways that my friends could understand. Given the temperament of my friends, and particularly Abraham, I also learned to manage disagreement. These lessons I also found very beneficial in the future.

***

EMP. My father placed great store in his friends. While he only mentions George and Abraham in his writings, he had many friends that he remained loyal to throughout his life and they to him.

The Trumans held a special place in his heart and mine. I cannot remember a time when they were not a central part of our lives and doings. Just as we considered the Pryors to be family, so did we consider the Trumans. Indeed, we referred to George and Catherine as aunt and uncle throughout my life, and their children became close friends as well. For myself, I cannot remember a time that the Trumans and their seemingly vast family were not a part of our lives. The Trumans reciprocated these feelings, and they were our most frequent visitors after our removal to the frontier.

On those rare instances when I traveled to Philadelphia on behalf of the family or business, the first instruction I always received was what wishes to convey to both George and Abraham. As it was considered somewhat perilous for a young woman to travel alone, I most frequently stayed with the Trumans when in Philadelphia. These events were all too infrequent, and I was accompanied by a chaperon on all occasions, but they were always memorable for one reason or another.

Philadelphia

For my father's part, I believe his single greatest regret in life was leaving his friends in Philadelphia. While we grew happy elsewhere, I know he thought of his friends frequently, wrote them as often as he could, and treasured the visits they made to Waterloo or those he made to Philadelphia to see them. On more than one occasion when I worked alongside my father, I would catch him with his eyes closed, seemingly distracted from the moment. When I queried him about these moments, he would inevitably remark that he had been thinking of George or Philadelphia—both of which claimed a special place in his heart.

I think one of the greatest joys of his life, and for him a fitting one, was that the M'Clintocks and Trumans would become one through marriage. While he was happy for me when I married and took much satisfaction with Burroughs, he was as jubilant as a quiet Quaker could be with the marriage of Mary to James Truman.

Chapter Three
Becoming a Member of the Society of Friends

My life in Philadelphia as an apprentice consisted of much more than just learning a trade and engaging in social intercourse with my companions; soon I began to explore the spiritual side of life.

Throughout my early years, religious matters meant little to me. Yes, I read the Bible faithfully and I believe acted in accordance with the dictates of the Christian faith, but I gave matters of the spirit little conscious thought. The fact that I had not sinned to any significant extent I owe more to my beloved mother than to any divine intervention.

At about the age of fifteen, however, I began to attend the same Meeting that the Bertrams attended on a fairly regular basis. At first, I confess, I went as much for the opportunity to make the acquaintance of young women in the area as for the spiritual sustenance. As I was quite shy at the time and my daily activities did not draw me near girls of my own age, I determined that going to Meeting would afford me that opportunity in an appropriate setting. While I did find that it was true I could become acquainted with girls of my age, it did not make me any less shy or tongue-tied in their presence. Meeting did not afford me great grace in the social sphere, but I soon found a joy and contentment in Meetings that I had not previously encountered.

At first, the idea of sitting in silence I found quite vexing. Prior to attending my first Meeting, I had received some direction on how to act (in truth, a great deal of direction on how to act and what not to do) and what to expect. No amount of preparation, however, could prepare me for my early experiences of sitting amongst a group of men and women—many of whom were well known and respected in the community—in silence while we waited for the word of the Spirit to descend upon us. To be clear, it was not time spent in total silence, as often an individual would rise and deliver a short message as the Spirit moved him or, on occasion, her. But as a young man, initially I found the extended silence to be unsettling in large part, I suspect, because I was waiting for a voice that did not come to me. Over time I became more at ease with the process of Meeting and settled into my own reverie and thoughts, and Meeting itself became a time of comfort for me.

Upon first making this spiritual quest, I remained greatly discomforted that I did not hear or sense the inner light and assumed it was some failing on my part. As a consequence I soon settled into a pattern of trying to clear my mind of extraneous thoughts, a pattern I have maintained to this day and one that seems to work for me. Words do not do that justice, but it seems as if I am able to assume a posture that allows peace to descend over me, allowing me to discern that which was not previously apparent.

During my early years of attending Meetings, I did little to concern myself with the inner workings of the Society, remaining content to use the time to my benefit and the time before and after to meet with friends and occasionally make new friends. I did not attend the Meetings for business or the other meetings that conducted the business of the Society. I did pay close attention to the words of others—marking those comments I concurred with and noting those

Becoming a Member of the Society of Friends

that I disagreed with. Often I would rush back to my room from Meeting and pore over the Bible in an attempt to understand the words I had heard as compared to the word of God contained in the Bible. Many times I was greatly distressed to discover that the Bible said one thing and honorable men said something quite different. Over time I came to the point of view that the Bible was not the final word of God, but that others could also hear God or hold differing viewpoints, and that was the natural order of religious affairs.

I kept my silence in Meetings for more than three years, although I attended regularly. The first time I ever spoke in Meeting was to rise and announce my intention to become a professed member of the Society of Friends, if they should have me. As a young man I often felt that this was the first truly free decision I had made in my life. And, while it has at times had its tribulations, it is a decision I have never regretted and one I hold to this day.

My announcement then led to a review of my life and a round of stringent interviews by the preparative committee. Over the period of several weeks, I was questioned about my faith, beliefs, and actions in order to discern whether or not I was acceptable to the Friends. While at times I wished it to be a simpler process, answering questions was a beneficial exercise for me as I was forced to clarify my positions and give significant thought to the implication of my decision. Ultimately, after due deliberation, I was cleared by the committee and at the age of nineteen I became a committed member of the Society of Religious Friends. While the circumstances of that commitment have changed over the years, I hold that I have honored it since.

***

EMP. While conditions changed over time and others would not agree, my father always considered himself a member of the Society of Friends, a Quaker through and through. I subscribe, as he does later, that his Orthodox friends are guilty of intolerance in this matter, as noted by the fact that his death was not marked to any great extent by any of the mainline Quaker publications, an unforgivable oversight in light of the entire honor he brought to the Society of Friends.

As for participation in Meeting, I remember my father as quite active, although he was obviously older by this time. Indeed it seemed to me that he spoke altogether too frequently and at some length, much to my embarrassment as a young girl who was conscious of what others thought.

I have no memory of either of my parents engaging in any form of prayer other than the occasional grace before a meal, but both were quite comfortable with silence and took great comfort from it. I queried my father once on this matter and he seemed to hold to the position that listening to the voice of God was far more important than speaking to God. He held that listening was the greater and harder skill, both in matters of faith and in human interactions. On this I believe he is correct and I have always tried to spend more time listening to others than I did in talking about myself.

***

Establishing a Business

Approaching adulthood, I continued my education with Moses and had advanced to the point that I was considered a master druggist and chemist. Achieving this level of proficiency meant that I was now an employee and received regular wages and responsibilities as such. Reaching the point that I was paid for my services marked another turn in the road for me, as I also assumed the responsibilities that came with having my own funds.

Attaining this level of learning also meant that I began to entertain visions of opening my own establishment, as I knew that I

Becoming a Member of the Society of Friends

both desired the independence and if I ever wanted to support my own family, I would have to take that step. Accordingly, I began to investigate the necessary steps to establishing my own emporium. Fortunately for me, and as was always the case, Moses was more than willing to provide good counsel in this endeavor, as he expected that all his apprentices would move on at some point in time. From our discussions I discerned that I would have to bring attention to three major areas: funding (for I did not possess the necessary capital to start a business), location, and clientele.

To my great benefit, I was able to secure the necessary funds in the form of loans from Moses and assorted family members. While the funds were not vast and assumed I would turn a profit in short order, they did provide me with the means to rent a suitable space and to secure an initial inventory of supplies. Likewise, a small number of local suppliers were willing to extend me credit for my start, which was of invaluable assistance. While I did not like the idea of credit, it was necessary to the endeavor. However, I resolved to repay my debts as soon as was humanly possible, even if that meant forgoing pleasures for myself. I have made conscious effort to maintain ties to those who supported me in my start, and whenever possible I have continued to do business with those who were my initial providers.

As to the question of location, I found this more troublesome. Certainly I did not wish to infringe on Moses' location or repay his kindness by encroaching on his customers, but I also knew that almost all his customers lived close to him. Accordingly, I secured a map of the city and against that map plotted the location of all the druggists I knew to be currently in operation. From that review and my knowledge of where in the city expansion was occurring, I quickly identified two or three areas that looked promising as to the size of the potential clientele and the lack of existing apothecary shops.

Using this knowledge, I then began to engage in a series of walking tours of the city during my free time in an attempt to identify a suitable building in which I could secure a space for both my business and my residence. In short order, I found such a space and reached agreement with the landlord on a suitable indenture. Thus began preparations to open my business, "Thomas M'Clintock, Druggist," at 107 South 9th Street. This establishment met my expectations and offered the advantage of additional living space should my family situation change in the future.

I began my preparations in early 1813, and after much effort I was able to open my establishment on the 15th day of fifth month in 1814. I shall long note that date as my day of independence.

Such was my haste to open my shop that it was only after all was prepared for when I realized I had no furniture of my own, and I had little or no idea about how to prepare food for myself as I had taken my meals with others to this point. I look back on this now with good humor, as normally I am a person who plans out his actions carefully. But in this case, I could not plan for what I did not realize I needed. Suffice it to say that I learned to provide food for myself and found a bed to sleep in, but I confess that the food I ate was not the most savory I had ever sampled. Nonetheless, I survived.

The first years were hard as I was both the proprietor and the sole employee. As such I carried the burden of all the duties of an apprentice and as a journeyman, and now as a master. If the store was to be open, supplies on hand, customers greeted, or cleanliness maintained, there was only one person responsible to ensure the task completed: myself. If I was to fail, there was no one liable other than myself. Fortunately for me, I was not overly burdened with clientele at first, and this allowed ample opportunity for the cleaning, arranging, and thinking that owning my own shop required. The latter was especially important for, while I had given much thought to the location of my business and the surrounding population, I had given almost no thought to attracting people to my establishment. This was something of a critical dilemma as I had created a first-class emporium but had few choose to use its services.

I commenced as diligently as possible to rectify that situation. Amid posting announcements and advertisements in the local journal, I also ordered a supply of cards printed with pertinent information about my establishment. These I handed out during my off hours by going from door to door introducing myself in the local community. Overcoming my shyness to engage in this door-to-door promotion was an exceedingly painful chore for me, but I recognized that it needed to be done. Ever so slowly, one at a time, people ambled into my store and, after a time, made purchases. I confess I was slow to repay the goodness of Mr. Bertram and my family, but after fourteen months I had repaid the initial loans, satisfied my creditors, and was able to put aside a little each month for my own use. It gave me ease of mind not to be beholden to someone else, and I found my nights were far more restful.

Without a companion to accompany me on this new stage of life, it was, I confess, something of a lonely time in my life. Should I depart from the store, I would lose potential customers, and as a consequence I spent the hours from sunup to sundown in my store. This left little time for my friends or other activities. With the exception of Meetings on Sunday and the rare other social event, I had little congress with my friends. Fortunately for me this was soon rectified, but for several years I felt as if I was a hermit alone with my thoughts in a cave.

***

EMP. Again, I believe my father gives himself short shift. Having done the same myself in starting my own business, I can attest to the countless difficulties that one must overcome when beginning a new venture. When I started my business, I had the good fortune to be supported by my parents both financially and emotionally, coupled with having my own resources to fall back on. To go it alone into a new venture meant untoward hours of work and personal sacrifice. To have been successful within a mere fourteen months is a tribute to Father's Herculean labors and the personal reputation he must have had in the local community.

While it was a fact in the world of commerce that one might be beholding to another for money or goods at some times, taking on credit was a major taboo to him. He avoided it wherever possible. While he shied away from borrowing monies from others, he did not hesitate to extend that courtesy to those in need. By his reckoning, allowing customers to purchase needed pharmaceuticals on credit both provided for the needs of others and, on a practical level, ensured that the customers would return to his store in the future to purchase additional goods.

My father's comments regarding his setting up his own household I find humorous. While he was fastidious to a fault around his store, his knowledge of the domestic arts was minimal. To my knowledge he was helpless in the kitchen and I have often wondered what he ate during those lean years. I know he was not picky about what he ate, which is a trait I have assumed he adopted when he suffered through his own cooking or boarded with others.

Chapter Four
Beginning a Family

Marriage

In mid-1818, a seemingly insignificant event occurred that changed my life for the better.

On an unseasonably warm day, an elderly gentleman stopped into my shop to inquire if I had any remedies for a severe headache. After asking a few questions regarding the nature of his malady, I provided him with a mixture of powders that I believed would provide him some relief. Before departing, he introduced himself as John Wilson of Burlington and explained that he was in Philadelphia in conjunction with his shipbuilding business. I had some knowledge of the Wilson family from their years in Delaware, so I asked that he stop in on his next visit and report on the results of my powders, and he agreed to do so.

To my great surprise, I again encountered John at the next Yearly Meeting. After exchanging greetings, he expressed his thanks for my assistance and indicated that my powders had provided much relief. As a way of further expressing his thanks, he invited me to share the noon meal with his family, and I accepted with gratitude, as I had no other plans or, for that matter, any means to obtain food for myself. That simple exchange marked a turning point for me that I could not have anticipated.

When I arrived at our agreed-upon meeting location, John introduced me with several kind words to his wife, Elizabeth, and two of his daughters, Margaret and Mary Ann. I enjoyed quite a lively time. The entire family was well-spoken, versed in the issues of the day, and they quite obviously shared my budding interest in the dilemma of slavery. I confess, however, that while I was keenly engaged in the conversation, I found myself more interested in the younger of the two daughters, Mary Ann, and to my surprise, I believed that she shared an interest in me. There was something in Mary Ann's nature that made me bold where usually I was quite retiring, and before departing from one another, I secured her permission to correspond with her. As was proper at those times, I also secured the permission of both John and Elizabeth to such an endeavor, and they graciously granted their agreement with the further pronouncement that should I wish to visit Burlington at some point in the future, they would be happy to have me as their guest.

Upon my return to my lodgings, I immediately drafted the first of what would be many letters to Mary Ann expressing my pleasure in meeting her. My initial boldness also gave vent to my sharing some of my history and hopes with her by way of an introduction. I posted the letter with much trepidation, as all my previous encounters with members of the opposite sex had led to nothing more than passing heartaches. To my immense surprise and pleasure, I received an almost immediate response from Mary Ann sharing both her delight in my epistle and returning the favor of discussing her history and hopes, all of which I found most entertaining and in alignment with my own ideas.

This initial encouragement, the first I had ever received from a woman, quickly led to a veritable torrent of letters flowing from my pen in which I espoused on various and sundry topics of inter-

Beginning a Family

est to me. To my eternal amazement Mary Ann responded in kind. Through this accumulating correspondence, I soon discerned that Mary Ann was a woman of intellect and refinement. And, as I discovered, she also possessed a sense of humor that served to balance my usually serious, more sober nature.

After several weeks of daily correspondence on my part, I cast my lot upon the waters and enclosed an inquiry in one of my letters asking as to whether or not I might call upon her in Burlington. To my immense pleasure, she responded with an invitation to visit Burlington and her family within the fortnight. By post I quickly accepted, and we made firm arrangements for a visit in the near future.

It was only after accepting the kind invitation that I realized I had no conception of how one was to conduct oneself in such a courting situation, for in my mind I had determined that I was indeed going to court Mary Ann with both honorable and serious intentions. To rectify this matter, I consulted with several of my friends as to proper conduct, but neither George nor Abraham was much assistance, as their experience in such matters amounted to no more than mine. It was only when I encountered James and Lucretia Mott at Meeting that I received some reassurance and assistance.

Lucretia offered counsel that I should let my actions speak of my intentions, which only served to deepen my confusion as I was not completely sure what that meant, although I knew my intentions were honorable. Sensing my confusion, James took me aside and, as usual, offered practical advice, indicating that I should plan to take small gifts for the family, be pleasant and helpful, and not leave Burlington until I had received Mary Ann's agreement to see her again. While I still remained comparatively in the dark as to the exact actions I should take, I found James's comments reassuring and sensible, for I knew that at minimum I could be helpful to the family.

On the agreed upon date I took the stage and ferry to Burlington to begin a new adventure in my life. Upon arriving at the Wilsons' home, it quickly became apparent that my anxieties were groundless as I was put at ease and made to feel as a welcome guest of the entire family. It was a congenial gathering, and I found that I had much in common with John. He had fought in the War of Revolution, as had my father and grandfather, and he was much interested in the cruelties of the slave trade. The latter he seemed to take most personally as a boat builder by trade, and he lived in fear that his creations had been used to transport human beings across the Middle Passage.

My courtship with Mary Ann moved with what seemed to me to be great slowness. Mary Ann and I swiftly discerned that we had a mutual interest in one another. Indeed, after several months of seeing one another and corresponding between times, we had reached an understanding that the bonds of matrimony were in our future. While reaching this decision was most pleasant for me, it did not lead directly to a wedding; first I hoped to secure John's consent and then, and even more importantly, both Mary Ann and I needed to secure the consent of the Burlington Meeting to our marriage.

Asking John for Mary Ann's hand was by far the easier task, as he deferred to Mary Ann's wishes in this matter, whose consent I had already secured. The concurrence of the Meeting was not as effortless a task as I had anticipated, for I was a stranger to Burlington and, as a result, found myself attending Meeting on a regular basis in Burlington to become known to the Elders and others. In truth, this was not an arduous endeavor, as it also gave me frequent opportunity to visit with Mary Ann.

On one of my visits to Burlington in the summer of 1819, while promenading with Mary Ann, she turned to me and remarked, "Thee has noticed that neither Margaret nor my mother any longer accompanies us on our walks?" In truth, I had not fathomed this as a matter of any import, but I nodded wisely in response. Mary Ann then explained that this was a sign that marriage had been accepted by all, including the Burlington Meeting. I received this communication with surpassing joy, and very indiscreetly we embraced while agreeing to be married as soon as arrangements could be made. While Quaker weddings are simple affairs, it was not until January that our union would take place.

Accordingly, on the 13th day of January in the year of our Lord 1820, I stood with Mary Ann before our friends at Burlington Meeting and we recited our vows to another. It was the best day of my life. I have never regretted for a moment my choice of bride or our decision to share life's journey with one another.

***

EMP. As was the habit of my parent's time, they spoke little of their courtship and romance, but I have always believed that theirs was true love. Never were they happier than when they were in the presence of one another. While not outwardly affectionate, as that would have been unseemly in the company of others, their smiles and laughter spoke volumes about their love. Oftentimes, and even into their old age, they would sit before the fire holding hands while reading—often aloud to one another. For all too brief a time in my own life, I shared their sentiments, so I speak from some perspective.

My father had small touches with my mother that struck all that knew him as notes of grace. While not a great enthusiast of works of fiction, he did love poetry and both read it for his own enjoyment and recited from memory when asked. In addition to the numerous religious tracts, abolitionist volumes, and other serious works kept around our home, my father maintained a goodly collection of poetic works. He especially enjoyed the works of Wheatley, Whittier (whom he knew personally), and in his later years Whitman. Shakespeare as well enjoyed a prominent place on my father's shelves.

After we moved to Waterloo, my father traveled far more often in the name of various causes. Whenever he would depart for a trip, he always left behind a note to my mother containing some lines of poetry from a wide range of authors in one shape or another professing his undying love. My mother, for her part, always looked for these notes, and on some occasions she would share them with us. On others, when asked, she would inform us that the note was not proper for young ears. I never saw those notes but always suspected they were of a more passionate nature.

I know that she reciprocated and tucked away her own scribbled notes and mementos in my father's luggage, as she was not a great writer and would sometimes ask for our assistance in this endeavor. As a consequence, some of her notes were of a more humorous nature than those of my father, but they both enjoyed the game.

Clearly my father thought this intimate communication was important, for when Mary and I decided to get married later in life, the only advice he ever gave our future husbands was to do something of the same. He did not require poetry, although Burroughs enjoyed it, but suggested small notes of endearment as a soothing step. To my knowledge both Burroughs and James heeded this advice, and it was much appreciated.

My father must have also learned when to let go from John Wilson, as he was most casual about matters when Mary and I were being courted by suitors. While he conversed with various suitors about issues of the day, which I believe was his way of checking their worth, he remained confident throughout in our judgment in matters of the heart.

***

Family

Mary Ann and I quickly set up housekeeping in the rooms abutting my establishment on 9th Street. It was, I confess, an adjustment

Beginning a Family

for me as a heretofore bachelor to share my home with another, but I found the change both welcome and pleasant.

We found our first months full of the trials and tribulations that those who are newly married face as we set up our home, transferred Mary Ann's Meeting membership to the Southern District, and made new friends and acquaintances as a couple. Fortunately for me, Mary Ann brought with her a number of comforts, not the least of which was furniture that quickly allowed us to establish a comfortable home and permitted the ease of having others join with us for social gatherings and discussions. In addition, her skills in the kitchen far surpassed my meager exposure to epicurean delights, and for the first time in my life I ate well.

We soon found ourselves seeing much of James and Lucretia, as well as establishing close ties with George Truman and Catherine Master, who would wed shortly. I found myself much enjoying the fact that our world was a broader one, enhanced by the grace that Mary Ann brought with her.

***

EMP. It is interesting to me to note that my father mentions James and Lucretia Mott several times early in his manuscript but never describes how they met; it is a story neither he nor my mother ever shared with me. I have always assumed that they met early on through some Quaker function, but I have no proof of that. I do know that they continued in one another's orbits for most of their lives.

***

All that I had found good and true in Mary Ann as we courted proved to be but the surface of all that was virtuous about her. In truth, I came to believe that Mary Ann was far smarter than I, particularly when it came to matters involving others. She was able to speedily judge the character of another and identify motivations for good and bad far earlier than I. I soon found that I could discuss any matter with her and receive wise counsel, and it became our habit to fully discuss the matters of the day before retiring to bed. Truly we became one as we shared common interests, agreed on the same course of action, and, on more than one occasion, laughed about the same things. Because of this, I believe that neither of us ever took a course of action or made a decision without first sharing it with the other.

Early on in our marriage it became evident that we, rather than I, existed in both the affairs of man and God. I found that having another to confide in, one who would listen to my concerns and worries, provided great benefit to me and I spent far fewer waking hours agonizing over the choices I would face in the morning.

As we grew increasingly familiar with one another, we also fell into a routine of reading together, and in this we also found agreement, as we discovered both solace and challenge in reading religious tracts as well as those that espoused on the various issues of the day, most notably slavery. In those days we found ourselves often engrossed in the words of Fox, Barclay, and Woolman while frequently perusing the passionate thoughts of Benezet and Lundy. In most instances, we would slowly read aloud to one another while we discussed each sentence or point. I found our exchanges both intellectually challenging and pleasant. As our family grew in number, we continued this habit with all who came into our sphere.

Our family soon changed both by birth and death. In the fall of 1820, it became apparent that Mary Ann was with child. During the fifth month of 1821, Mary Ann delivered our firstborn, Elizabeth, both safely and without undue discomfort. It was shortly after the birth of Elizabeth that Elizabeth Wilson, Mary Ann's mother, came to join our household as John had passed away after a brief illness. While I mourned the loss of John, as he had become a true friend,

Beginning a Family

the addition of both Elizabeths to our home brought much joy and respite.

The addition of Elizabeth Wilson was particularly helpful as neither Mary Ann nor I had much experience with young children, and her counsel in child rearing as well as her assistance in maternal matters was a boon to us both. With most of my attention being paid to the growth of my business and other concerns, having another adult in the home was a great help in all domestic matters. This became particularly true when we once again added to our expanding family with the birth of Mary Ann in 1822, then Sarah in 1824, Julia in 1826, and at last Charlie in 1829.

I found that there was much comfort to be had in holding a small child, and as they grew older I also rediscovered the playful joys of childhood. All was forgiven; all pains were forgotten with the unknowing smile of a small loved one.

The joy we felt with the birth of our son was greatly tempered by the sudden death of Julia. It seemed as if one day she was a bright, happy child and the next day she was gone. Our grief consumed us for some time as both Mary Ann and I were overcome with the loss and the feeling that we had somehow failed as parents. While time and the presence of God heal all wounds, at the time that was small consolation to our breaking hearts. I confess that poor Charlie may have suffered the most due to our lack of attention, but fortunately Elizabeth and his sisters were able to fill the breach. While eventually we were able to put memory of Julia in the back of our minds, the shock of that event has never left me. To the present time I have carried with me a great fear for the health and safety of my family, always trying to keep them near to me and under my protection.

Fortunately for us, we were blessed with another addition to our family, and in 1831, another daughter, whom we named Julia in honor of her departed sister, joined our family. Our family was complete and remained together as a unit until the 1850s.

The Memories of Thomas M'Clintock

***

EMP. I remember my childhood as a happy one. As we lived in the same structure where my father maintained his business for many of those years and had other adults in the house, it seemed that there was always someone there to take care of us and see that we were behaving correctly. My parents were certainly not rigid in their child rearing. While they expected us to behave in an appropriate manner and treat others with respect, as long as we met those standards they were not harsh or demanding, indeed just the opposite. I remember us as laughing often, playing childish games and always having an open lap to hop up into.

What discipline there was, and there was not much, clearly fell to the purview of my mother. My father, gentle soul that he was, was constitutionally unable to raise either his hand or voice against another. I confess that we probably took great advantage of this kindness, as all of us knew early on that the safest place when we had committed some minor transgression was to be near my father. Oh, he would talk to us about our grave misdeeds, but he was unable to do so without a twinkle in his eye or some candy within easy reach.

They were serious about our studies. Each of us began to learn our letters prior to being sent to school. As soon as we were of age, we were trundled off to the nearest Quaker school. In addition to reading with us at the end of each day, they established the habit of reviewing our lessons with us as well. While both were interested in this task, my father in particular seemed to take much pleasure in this, often remarking on how much more we were learning than he did at the same age. On occasion I would find him reading one of my lessons for his own pleasure or edification, mumbling to himself in either agreement or disagreement.

Beginning a Family

My grandmother, Elizabeth, after whom I was named, I mark with great fondness. Although she passed on relatively early in my life, she brought a great calmness and sense of serenity to the household. It was from her that I first learned my letters. And from her I gained the early sense that all was possible.

Chapter Five
Public Life

As my business became settled and ample to meet our financial needs, I had time to become active in the world around me. I say that with some caution as I tried to stay true to Quaker prohibitions on being in the world but nonetheless I ventured into other realms. Some of those were part of the Society of Friends; others were distinctly in the world of men and women, politics, and the larger society.

As I write these words, I speak of myself, but to be clear, all that I said or did was with the able support of Mary Ann. For a variety of reasons, not the least of which that Mary Ann did not cherish the idea of putting pen to paper or speaking in public, I generally took the lead. But all that I ever said or wrote was done with the blessing and support of my chief advisor and confidant, Mary Ann. She has always been, and continues to be, my source of solace, serenity, and wisdom above all others.

Most notably among our social activities Mary Ann and I entered into the orbit that surrounded Elias Hicks of New York and the controversy that seemed to engulf Green Street Meeting. I had first heard Elias's ministrations on one of his visits to Philadelphia sometime after 1815. While I made little note of his initial comments, I subsequently became in much agreement with his views on God and the Quaker relationship to God and worship. It was my belief, and Mary Ann's, that he spoke the truth and pointed the Society in the correct direction in keeping with the works of George Fox and others. Certainly his views were in accordance with my own study of Fox and the Scriptures.

When I first met Elias, he was already quite elderly but still carried himself in an erect, virile manner. His speaking voice was calm, deliberate, and measured but altogether pleasing and compelling. It was my honor to name him as a friend and to engage in an active correspondence with him and his other associates. I did so at some risk as, by this time, he had already become the source of strong feelings among the more substantial members of the Society of Friends. But I found that he spoke the truth, and my inner voice required that I follow that truth. Little did I know that my support of Elias would thrust me into the center of rancorous debate and acrimony among the Friends and friends.

***

EMP. The details my father shares about my mother are true to my experience with her. For whatever reason, perhaps just exhaustion, my mother did not enjoy writing letters or corresponding with others. While she devoured the letters from others and always had comments on what they wrote, it was a source of much merriment and glee within the family when she actually would write someone. We teased her without letup on those occasions, and it is to her credit that she took our mirth with good humor.

My father's relationship with Elias was no secret. I was told that Elias had been a visitor in our house, something my parents took great pride in, but I have no memory of that. I do know that his cousin, Edward, stayed with us on several occasions when visiting in the area.

Public Life

***

Shortly after I exchanged some correspondence with Elias regarding the publication of his sermons for the general public, it became apparent that some members of the Society viewed his opinions as both inimitable with the beliefs of the Quakers and, in the extreme, denying the divinity of Jesus. Lo, these many years I have held my tongue in the interest of harmony and in the spirit of the inner light. I have never denied another person the right to a view of the truth. Indeed I have prided myself on the ability to see both sides of an argument. But now, after many years have passed, I would speak what the heart has held quiet.

To me the conflict was a simple one. While there was much agreement on each side, there were some differences on particular matters of religious doctrine. These differences, combined with the vain desire to control others, ultimately led to a rendering of the spirit of unity. On the religious side, it seems that there were two central concerns: whether the Bible was the literal word of God or open to the interpretation of others, and whether the divinity of Jesus was a fact.

The question of the biblical interpretation became a matter of much discord, while the question about Jesus' deity was used by the other side to attack the teachings and character of Elias. As to the first matter, the side that came to be known as Orthodox seemed to hold that the Bible was the final word of God, the one true description of behavior and orthodoxy. It is my firm opinion that much of this position reflected the currents of the day and was done, in part, to make the Quakers seem more acceptable to the other Christian faiths. It is my belief and, perhaps the belief of many who became known as Hicksites, that this position ran contrary to the original teaching of George Fox and others who were critical in shaping the thought of the Society of Friends. As I read Fox, it was eminently clear to me that he believed that the word of God was open to the interpretation of each worshipper and that faith, belief, and understanding could change over time with one's experience of God. The understanding of God was not static, but a living experience that could and should change over a period of time.

The position of individual interpretation combined with the belief that works were more important than words served as the core of my position. From this position I held to the stance that Elias correctly interpreted the belief structure of the Quakers. As a consequence, where he went, or as events would have him forced to go, I would follow. As a matter of the Society of Friends discipline, I believe this was the heart and marrow of the issue. It was an issue that ultimately was resolvable with goodwill and intent. Indeed, had we put goodwill and good intent to the seeking of the way, all was possible. But these two characteristics were sadly lacking.

The matter of Jesus' divinity and Elias' stance was more troubling. During the long travails it seemed that the Orthodox were intent on attacking Elias' beliefs as heresy. They were seemingly convinced that if they could damage the man, they would damage the truth that he spoke. Repeatedly the Orthodox threw down the gauntlet that Elias had denied the divinity of Jesus, forcing him to spend much time and energy defending himself, clarifying his position, and making claims to Orthodox views of Christ. The whole matter was but a feint designed to hide the views of a few behind attacks on another; for it was no matter, as true Quakers were each open to their own experience of God and Jesus. Whether one believed Jesus to be the son of God or not was in truth of no consequence to those who believed in God, as all roads ultimately converged on God. The vain popinjays of Quaker hierarchy used the question as a cudgel to obscure the futility of their position.

In truth, their view of Elias' beliefs was, in the main, correct. While he countered their arguments and accusations vigorously in both word and print, my own correspondence with him would seem to indicate he had doubts—doubts which I share. I am inclined toward the position that God is one and, in that sense, I am in agreement with the Unitarians, especially Theodore Parker. Whether one believes Jesus to be divine or whether salvation comes with acceptance of Jesus Christ seems to be of little matter when compared with how one lives their life. How we put into practice our faith in God, our treatment of our fellow man, and behavior on a daily basis is of far greater importance. I cannot believe that if one is venal, base, and malicious toward his fellow man but believes in Jesus Christ, the belief in Jesus will outweigh all else in relation to the prospect of eternal life.

If all that is so, then what caused the vile schism among Quakers? Certainly questions of religion can make the heart throb with passion, but in this matter I believe the cause was the vain need of a few to impose their will on the rights of many. For the Orthodox part, the sense of the elders was deemed to be more important than the sense of the Meeting. The elders, the Meeting for Suffering, and the control of the business of various meetings was more important to the brethren associated with Jonathan Evans and others than questions of faith or belief.

At the marrow it was control over others that shaped the great divide. A small band of wealth holders believed that they knew what was best for others and that they alone possessed access to the truth. I hold those who would have maintained power as guilty of intolerance and an unwillingness to be open to the Spirit and to be, in large measure, accountable and responsible for the division. Further, I measure that no man, elder or clergy, has any greater insight into the truth than another. To hold the contrary as one's position is to place oneself in the place of God and this is an abomination. While only God will judge the truth, I believe right is on my side.

I have digressed into reverie as to what caused the split between Orthodox and Hicksite. In truth, the actual breach was long years in coming. While Elias continued to preach his message and suffer the slings and arrows of his detractors, there were those of us who both supported him and actively defended his views. Seemingly centered at Green Street Meeting, where Abraham Lower, I, and others joined with like-minded supporters such as William Poole in Wilmington, we raised the banner of support for the beliefs of Elias as we discerned that he spoke the proper message of the Society.

In truth, and as we were accused by the Orthodox, we did meet on occasion over those years to plan and debate courses of action—usually in response to what was anticipated in the way of action from our erstwhile Orthodox friends. However, I would hold that the ultimate cause of disunion and the fault for it lay with those who chose to cling onto power over all other principles. Yes, we forced the question of division, but we were more than prepared to find a sense of the total body. But alas, that was not to be.

After many years of debate, attempted compromise, and mutual messages of vituperation, it became clear that a division into two separate Quaker realms was in order. I much rued the day that this occurred, as it resulted in the loss of friends, including the good Moses Bertram, as well as proving harmful to my business. Many of my former customers who chose the Orthodox side ceased to do business with me and with others who chose the path of Elias. Altogether it was a time of much suffering and grieving over a loss that could have been prevented if others had but opened their hearts. Little did I know that what seemed like a simple affair of religious doctrine would soon extend its reach into the court system of the land as each side staked claims on their right of ownership of various Meetings and holdings throughout the land of the Quakers. It was a painful time and one that remains an open, sore wound until this very day.

Public Life

All was not gloom and darkness as I ventured into the outer sphere. Certainly my increasing family, now including my niece Sarah, brought me great joy and happiness.

I also began to put pen to paper as I shared my thoughts on a variety of issues with the rest of the world. Prior to my marriage, I had, on occasion, jotted down some thoughts on different topics for my own use primarily in the recipe book in which I kept my chemical preparations. My first formal foray into the published word included short pieces that I had submitted to either the Friend or the Berean, which offered commentary on various aspects of either Quaker thought or the controversy caused by Elias. Early on I used the pen name of Leland, but I soon abandoned this practice and submitted all my works under my own name. I became convinced that if I was going to share my thoughts, it was only correct to do so under my own identity. Using the name of another seemed to be hiding behind their skirts.

I entered the fray on the issue of the observance of the Sabbath with some thoughts that were deemed suitable for publication by Joseph Rakestraw and others. Consequently, my first book, *Essays on the Observance of the Sabbath,* was set in print in 1822. While Lucretia has always accused me of taking my stance because of business concerns, I thought the essays were well reasoned, and I confess to a good deal of pride in seeing my name in print.

Not all of my publishing efforts were confined to my own written word. It was also my pleasure and honor to serve as a part of the editorial group that put together the first complete collection of Fox's work. I found this process very satisfying and educational as it continued my study and scholarship. While my contribution was small, the effort was enriching for me. The study of Fox's words also served to verify the truth that Elias and others spoke and to solidify my own thinking on the matter.

The Memories of Thomas M'Clintock

***

EMP. As I was raised as a Hicksite and encouraged always to speak my own mind, I can add very little about these prior events regarding the schism. My father was a man of much integrity, and I believe he always acted in a way that was consistent with his view of the truth. I can remember distinctly his response to a question from Giles Stebbins when he said, "I must speak the truth and abide the consequences." I believe he acted in a manner consistent with this throughout his life. These events speak to his integrity and a willingness to voice his dissent in matters of injustice.

Of the feeling that existed between the Hicksites and Orthodox, I can speak more directly. Even when I ran my store in Philadelphia, years after we returned from Waterloo, feelings ran quite high. It was not unusual for a matron who might be browsing in my store to inquire if "thee were Hicksite" or if "thee were Orthodox." I lost few customers over this, as I was neither by this time, but the fact that the question remained over so many years spoke to the intensity of emotion that still surrounded that event. While I made little of it, I would also note that there were still those who crossed the street to avoid someone they knew was of the other persuasion.

My father's name also invoked those passions. While I did not use the M'Clintock name, there were those who used it either with great pride or distain, depending on their perspective. The reactions spoke to his active role in the controversy.

Even more than sixty years later the anger among people was almost palpable. I despaired that the breach would ever be healed and had little hope that people of goodwill would ever find common ground.

While my father would not use the word, I considered him a scholar, in particular on biblical matters and the writings of the Society of Friends. When I read his works I was continually im-

pressed by the range of sources he used in his writings and the power of his thoughts. I know others such as Lucretia also thought well of him in this area.

***

Perhaps it is vanity, but I have felt moved to share my thoughts with others after those initial stumbling attempts. Since my first endeavors I have continued to write and publish some of those efforts. I have found the writing process as both a way to clear my mind and a way to minister to others. Much of that writing has been the result of my growing involvement with the horror of slavery; however, it is ironic to me that in my later years I have returned to original themes such as the Sabbath that I wrote about long ago.

As I began to write, a good part of what occupied my mind, in addition to various and sundry religious themes was the plight of the slaves. When Mary Ann and I joined together, one of our bonds was a shared commitment to the injustice of owning another person. We spend much time reading the works of Benezet, Woolman, and other early Quakers who struggled with the notion of slavery in the Society. We, like they, found that holding another in bondage was in opposition to the tenets of the Quakers. We also began to gain greater exposure to the thinking of those who were facing the problem of slavery. Both Mary Ann and I had members of the family who were early members of the Pennsylvania Abolition Society. Likewise, through my association with Moses, I had been exposed to the mutterings of the colonizers.

At first I was somewhat taken with the thoughts behind the colonization movement, as I saw it as a potential resolution to what seemed to be an insurmountable problem. However, through the efforts of Benjamin Lundy and the example set by James Forten, Richard Allen, and others, I came to see that each of us—regardless of color—should have the same rights in our native country. I later discovered in discourse with Richard Allen that many others also struggled with this dilemma. I resolved, therefore, to set my efforts against the enslavement of others and the unnatural bondage of one man to another. Mary Ann and I reached this position through much thought, prayer, and consultation with cherished friends. Reaching a decision to oppose slavery required little thought as the institution was and had been abhorrent to me. Taking action to openly oppose it, however, required more reflection.

Personally I was troubled by the treatment of slavery in the Bible and the contradictions contained therein. Much of the Bible seemed to condone slavery in fact, if not in action. But the teachings of Jesus and my own reflection seemed to both deny the right of slavery and compel one to action. Within the Society of Friends, this was not an altogether popular course of action, as many believed that involvement with anti-slavery efforts contradicted the teachings of Fox to not be in the world. However, I was swayed on my course through the counsel of Elias and others to hold true. And I believe I have done so through the long battle of ridding our land of this curse.

Out of this dialogue and through the close reading of Woolman, Benezet, and the like, some of my associates, including James Mott and George Truman, joined me in resolving to take action. After much thought and reflection we discerned that a course of action that we could all support, and one that might have an impact on the slaveholders and slave merchants, was to deny our support of such products produced by slave labor. While we were small in number, we believed that we could have a broad reach and affect the pocketbook of the slave mongers. As a consequence, James, others, and I formed the Free Produce Society of Pennsylvania, whose intent was to encourage other merchants to rid their shelves of products made by slave labor and to encourage our customers to do the same.

I do not know what impact we had, but I have held true to those principles throughout my time in business. For me this was a small step, but for others, such as James, devotion to these principles meant changing one's line of business. I have always had much respect for James in his determined willingness to take such a step and, in doing so, risk his livelihood.

***

EMP. To my knowledge my father always held true to the principles espoused by the Free Produce group. Certainly when we moved to Waterloo this was the case and his open avowal of this position often caused friction with potential customers, at least at first.

As a young person, I found the discussion of slavery, and reading that I was required to do on it, somewhat tedious. I realize now how much truth there was in it and how important it was in shaping my own life. While the cause of the slave was central to my parents, my reading closely linked the plight of the slave with status of women in our country. Both of my parents had strong opinions on these matters, but they let us choose our own course freely. Certainly they would discourse with us on our points of view and offer contrary positions but, in the end, we were allowed our own direction. This was abundantly true when Charlie went off to fight in the war. My parents were quite torn about this matter as it violated many beliefs they had long maintained, but they believed he was a man of free will and choice.

***

It is frequently strange how opening one door may lead one down another path. As part of the advocacy of Free Produce, I encountered through James Mott a brusque, direct businessman who would have a major influence on my life.

One day while visiting with James at his establishment, I chanced to meet a man from the hinterlands of western New York. Richard Hunt was in town to conduct business with James and we were briefly introduced to one another. Little did I know that that chance encounter would lead to a long association and a merger of our families by marriage.

This experience further opened my eyes in other ways as well. While I had longtime business dealings with the free colored population of Philadelphia, the founding of the Free Produce Society marked my first interactions with members of the African race as co-equals. I found it an altogether pleasurable experience. I judged Richard Allen and others to be upright citizens with all the appropriate intellect to compete successfully in the world. Through my exposure to Bethel Church, I resolved that I would never treat another human being differently based on race, and I believe I have held true to that as all have been welcome in our home and at our table. This stance has subjected me to the scorn of others, but I believe that it was consistent with the teachings of Jesus and his espousal of the golden rule and his dictates to "love your neighbor as yourself."

Those small steps on a road of decision and small actions set me on a course that consumed the better part of my life. I resolved that I would in action, thought, and deed oppose the very existence of slavery in any form throughout the land. In these endeavors I was much aided by Mary Ann and other friends and associates. My friendship with George Truman allowed me to take a trip with him into New York to gain additional perspective on the discussions in other Meetings and venues. Likewise, my association with Elias led me to Benjamin Lundy, which in turn led me to the sainted Garrison.

As I look back on the journey to Garrison, I realize now that I was well prepared to take the leap of faith to his moral suasion. Mary Ann and I had done the reading, moved through other forms of abolition, and rejected them, coming to the realization that the fight for abolition, by its nature, must be blind to color.

I have been honored to be an intimate associate of William Lloyd Garrison's for neigh onto forty years, first meeting him through my

Public Life

association with Benjamin Lundy. While we have had our disagreements over the years on matters of policy, or in some cases over William's more extreme stances, we have remained true to one another. I have supported him through my voice, defended him where it was needed, and in all ways stood with him in his single-minded determination to free slaves posthaste.

Of all those I have known over the years, Garrison was unique in his zealotry for the cause, at times to the detriment of his health and family. He remained, throughout his life, a lightning rod for the slings and arrows of the rabble that stood in opposition to those who would free the slaves. I know of no other individual, other than Frederick, who so consistently demonstrated bravery and fearlessness in the face of mobs and rowdies. My only regret during my long collaboration with him was my inability to accompany him to London in 1840, but finances and not philosophy was the barrier to that event.

Garrison himself burst to the forefront with the publication of the *Liberator* in 1831 and his call for the immediate emancipation of the slaves. His clarion call to action was most compelling and forthright. Early on we became subscribers, and in the later years it was my pleasure to serve as an agent of the *Liberator* in western New York. Within our circle in Philadelphia, he found ready supporters among my friends and those I had continued involvement with over Free Produce. In particular the free colored population of Philadelphia provided both financial and moral support to Garrison's call.

I can well remember the startling simplicity and directness of Garrison's call for immediate emancipation. His voice rang like a beautiful bell carrying a message of truth. If slavery was an abomination, if it was a sin, if it was immoral, then a just nation and people would end it now. Not tarrying for a gradual solution, not uprooting citizens of our country for transport to another world, but ending that immoral trade here and now—that was his stance.

The heartfelt, passionate simplicity of his message consumed Mary Ann and me. No more would we linger with the thoughts and imperfections of the past. Our course was set and has remained true until the recent War Between the States and the ultimate resolution of what many referred to as the "peculiar institution."

To be sure, most of our involvement with Garrison occurred after our departure from Philadelphia to the remote parts of New York. Both Mary Ann and I were aware of the ferment surrounding the establishment of the American Anti-Slavery Society in 1833. Indeed, I attended several sessions but business limited my involvement. Most of what we heard of the events was relayed to us by the Motts, Lucretia taking a most active role in the proceedings even though her participation was limited by her sex. Little did I know at that time how much the issue of one's sex and the attendant rights as a result would also figure into our future.

Indeed, Lucretia's exclusion from those proceedings, although she was allowed to speak directly, led to her organizing the Philadelphia Female Anti-Slavery Society (PFASS). Just as Mary Ann and I were compelled by the cause of the slaves, so were James and Lucretia. As in all things, however, Lucretia carried belief into action.

Lucretia has been deservedly much honored over the years by all that have encountered her. Her voice has consistently belied her diminutive stature, consistently calling for justice and confronting the illogic of others. We have known her over the years as a caring friend, engaging companion, and the fine hand behind many activities and connections. Lucretia had, and has, a superb ability to goad others into action while allowing each actor to believe that he or she took action directly themselves. In short, she possesses an unrecognized subtly that allows her to accomplish much that she is not given credit for.

This was much the case with the founding of the PFASS. In very short order after the men's convention, Lucretia had called together a group of like-minded women, both white and colored, to discuss what action they should take. While I shall always believe that Lucretia knew the answer to her proposed inquiry, she allowed the events to run their course with the resulting PFASS.

Mary Ann was intimately involved in the planning and discussions, which greatly pleased her. In the end, she, along with others, served on the committee that drafted the charter of the PFASS and much of its sentiments. This experience, along with the organizing of the Female Anti-slavery Society, served her in great stead in some of her future endeavors. Much like me, Mary Ann has long been comfortable working behind the scenes, lending her enormous talents as needed to various causes without the desire for recognition or a leading role.

Little did I anticipate the resistance we and others would face when confronting the evils of slavery. Much did I admire the bravery of those who faced down unruly mobs, often at great peril to themselves. It seemed that every time Garrison or another would speak out in public forums, they were met with mobs of young toughs often goaded on by otherwise responsible citizens. It appeared that mobs ruled the day, and I feared not only for the safety of my fellow men but for the very fabric of our society. Little did I know that my own daughter would face those perils herself in the city of brotherly love.

As I reflect back on the period of the twenties into the early thirties, it was a period of both spite and spirit. The pompous arguments of self-centered men whose wealth they deemed gave them more worth in the eyes of God was offset by the simple brilliance and high mindedness of numerous reformers, both white and colored. In the main, I believe I came through this period as a better person. My ideas were tested, I discerned where my true path lay, and I found that truly Mary Ann and I functioned as one. Much of the life that lay before me was formed in those years as I found that I could present myself to the world, hold true to my beliefs, and be heard by others. In a way it could be said that I found my voice, both in the spoken word and in print, but more to the point, I discovered from whence that voice emanated.

***

EMP. In many ways it is impossible to separate my parents from Garrison as they were true and ardent believers in him personally and the cause he espoused. While they disagreed with him on some matters of policy, particularly on his later advocacy of secession or in his treatment of Frederick, I never heard them utter a cross word about him. More to the point, they were frequent defenders of him both in print and word.

Personally, I always found William charming. During ours years in Waterloo he was a frequent visitor in our home, and he was a delightful companion. While he held strong views, he was willing to listen to the opinion of others and, in fact, seemed to take great pleasure in debate. With a small smile on his face, he would take on the most extreme views to incite discussion among others. I often thought he enjoyed the process, the give and take of debate, even more than the resolution of the issue. Even as a young girl, he would honor my opinion to the same degree that he would others who had more years of experience and distinction. It was the mark of almost all who graced our door, and Garrison was no exception, that voices were not raised in anger no matter how much disagreement there might be.

Of the events my father speaks of concerning his involvement in the movement, I knew very little at the time for I was young and not burdened with the issues of adults. I do remember seeming flurries of activity in which my father, and to a lesser extent my mother, would engage in deep conversations of a serious nature, but I was not aware of what they spoke on other than to note it must have been important. I do remember a stream of visitors, some from out of town, who would come to engage my father in private discussions. Likewise, on many nights my father ventured out for unknown purposes after the evening meal to return long after I had gone to bed. I believe now that those conversations must have been in regard to the coming Hicksite/Orthodox split, but I cannot verify that fact.

Several themes do emerge, however, which continued throughout my life with my parents. I was aware that my father wrote a great deal. Usually it was correspondence with others, but on various occasions he would remark that he was working on something of more import that required his concentration. This was his way of asking for privacy, which was difficult for us children who were both exuberant and often confined in a small house.

My father was something of a mutterer, often talking to himself as he worked or read the works of another, remarking into the air "this is good" or more often "bad, bad, bad." He would many times express an opinion aloud, which he would later change for one reason or another. I often thought that he was thinking out loud to test how his thoughts sounded, but I never asked him about this other than to take it as a sign that he was engaged with deep thoughts about a matter. In particular, when he disagreed with something he read, the volume and frequency of his vocalizations would increase at a dramatic rate. As children, whenever we heard him discourse about the illogic or reasoning contained in a piece, we could anticipate he would soon take his pen in hand to refute some poor soul's arguments.

I find his comments about his awakening regarding the capabilities of the colored population to be particularly enlightening. It seems, as I read his comments, that this represented a change for him in both thought and action. For myself, I cannot remember a time in which black men and women were not welcome in our home. My own activities in Philadelphia brought me into contact with both the Fortens and Purvises, both in our home and on occasion theirs, although no note was made of this. I always assumed that this was the way one interacted with other human beings and that race was not an issue. Certainly my parents represented this same action throughout my life with them. Particularly after we moved to Waterloo, but even before, numerous colored citizens graced both our table and our beds.

This was the normal course of events for us, but I realize now it was not standard practice for all. There were numerous times that some high-minded reformer would grace our table expounding at some length on the injustice of slavery while at the same time making vile comments about the capability of the African. These comments I never heard from those associated with Garrison, but they were heard in our home. I can remember distinctly the discomfort this caused my parents as they inevitably countered these comments vigorously. While conversations of an intellectual nature abounded in our home, along with much difference of opinion, these comments regarding race my parents believed to be unfounded, base, and, in the main, an expression of ignorance on the part of the speaker. They could not tolerate such expressions without presenting their own contrasting position. I believe they spoke not necessarily to convert another, but as witnesses to what they believed to be truth.

My own experience supported their position. One could not talk with Frederick Douglass, Jermain Lougen, Harriet Jacobs, or Harriet Purvis without realizing that these were people of rare intellect and capability. Nor could one long talk with Truth or Tubman without noting their bravery and fearlessness, which often surpassed all others regardless of race. Certainly not all were as capable as they were, but then not all whites were as capable as Garrison, the Motts, or my parents. It is an ignorance I have fought against

Public Life

throughout my life, both through the example of my parents and on my own.

Of my mother's experience with the early anti-slavery efforts, she said very little other than to remark that it was helpful with some of the events that subsequently transpired in Seneca Falls. I have often thought that my mother was not given her due as a stalwart of reform. While my father always recognized her abilities and praised her contributions, others did not make that observation. In her own right she was extremely competent, a recognized minister, well-read, and could be well-spoken when she chose to be. I have encountered many accomplished and famous women over the years and she remains my model for womanhood. I hold her memory very close to me and think of her often.

***

All was not contentious and great issues. As my public life and the affairs of the day unfolded, the normal vicissitudes of life continued. My business prospered and a steady stream of clientele graced my establishment on 9th. While the Quaker schism had some impact on my business through the loss of old customers, I gained new customers due to the split as well as many of the Hicksite persuasion gracing my door in a show of support and mutual fellowship. At least until the early thirties there were few worries in providing for our expanding family. As well, both Mary Ann and I remained immersed in the activities of Green Street Meeting. The Meeting remained the focal point of both our spiritual and social lives, as we found many congenial friends from among the members.

However, as the thirties moved forward, we found ourselves reconsidering our choices and options. The area in which we lived had become an increasing bastion of Orthodox Friends, which in turn caused an ever greater discomfort. Accordingly we resolved to explore other locales that might prove to be more amenable to both our religious affiliation and my business. After due deliberation, we decided to move to a more congenial spot north of the area in which I had established my business and we had maintained our home. While the move was disruptive, particularly to the children who felt they were leaving their friends, we resolved that it was the best thing for us. And so it proved, at least in the short term.

Events, however, soon proved otherwise, and shortly we would embark on another journey that would take us far from friends and family.

Chapter Six
To Waterloo

After several years in the northern portions of Philadelphia, events began to conspire that caused us to reconsider our decision to remain there. While in the main we had a pleasant home, a reasonably successful business, and congenial surroundings, other circumstances slowly intruded that caused us to consider a second move to another location outside of Philadelphia. Like many events of this nature, no one fact initiated this consideration. Rather it was the seeming confluence of a number of occurrences that led to this decision. I shall enumerate some of those reasons, as it was a wrenching choice to uproot from familiar faces. Chronicling this helps to put my mind at ease as I still question the decision after all these years. Many were the nights that I wrestled with the choices I faced in the still quiet that occurred after others were asleep.

For the most part I would say it was a decision about my trade. While I have never put the pursuit of wealth above all else, indeed my daughters would believe I have ignored it, I have always been aware of the need to provide for my family. And as the 1830s began to slip by, my business began to suffer. It was not an immediate downturn, and I was still able to provide for my family's needs, but it was a concern. My regular clientele became less frequent, and even those who did grace my doorstep complained about constraints they were under. I did not believe that my business was at risk of failure, but I began to consider whether or not there were greener pastures to explore. I know that all who undertake commerce face various cycles of feast and famine, but I had always assumed that my business was somewhat immune to those downturns as I catered to a basic need. When my customers refrained from attending to their health, I knew that matters were serious.

Mary Ann and I had many long discussions regarding this matter. In addition to my discomfort with the state of the store, she added to the list her growing dissatisfaction with the affairs of the Society of Friends. She felt more acutely than I the effects of the schism and recoiled at the notion that former friends now shunned her in the streets. Their lack of grace reflected badly on them, but it was disconcerting particularly to one as sensitive as Mary Ann. We reached no resolution but continually discoursed on the choice to go or stay. Like many, we wondered if there was greater opportunity in the West, but a move such as that felt like a step into the great unknown. It was a step we were not willing to take.

Then circumstances and events came together and provided resolution, or at least a choice. Upon the death of one of my uncles, my niece Sarah had come to live with us in 1829. While the circumstances were sad, she was a welcome addition to our family being just slightly older than Elizabeth and Maggie. She filled a void in our family that had been missing since the death of Elizabeth Wilson, as she was a joyous young woman who proved to be a boon companion for the girls. As chance would have it, however, she also proved to be attractive to eligible bachelors who were seeking wives. And so, in the course of events, who should come calling to inquire about Elizabeth but Richard Hunt. Apparently he had come to Philadelphia to do business with James and, as he freely confessed, to seek a wife as his had recently passed away.

To Waterloo

I was much disconcerted by this, as my own experience with courting was much different. Now, in addition to my own inexperience in matters of romance, I had the responsibility for the well-being of another, as Sarah was in my charge. Suddenly, and much too soon, I was thrust into the role of being a parent and having another wishing to take her away from me, for I was quite fond of Sarah. To his credit, Richard was clear in his intentions from the outset and very willing to take my lead. My position on the matter, as it was in many things, was to immediately seek Mary Ann's advice and counsel.

To have Richard, who was a good deal older than Sarah—actually closer to my age—and not a practicing Quaker courting Sarah was an added burden for our lives. While there was much in Richard's favor as he was settled and wealthy, it was clear that should the courtship progress to marriage, Sarah would be disowned from Meeting. Mary Ann's advice in the matter, while citing the marriage of my own parents, was to let nature take its course and to rely on Sarah's own good judgment. Accordingly we chaperoned Richard and Sarah during his initial visit to Philadelphia and agreed that they could continue to correspond with one another.

Richard was a very direct man of few words and, I confess, used to getting his way. During his initial visit he used every free moment, or so it seemed to me, to pursue his courtship with Sarah. While their time together was brief, there was ample opportunity for them to become acquainted. I do not think that Sarah found his ministrations unwanted and, indeed, I found that I liked and respected him quite a good deal myself. It was abundantly clear from the first visit that Richard was not going to take the long path to matrimony.

Richard continued his courtship from a distance quite vigorously as well. Scarcely a day went by that Sarah did not receive a letter from him or some small token expressing his adoration. I have never had much interest in the military sciences, but from a distance it would appear that he was waging a persuasive campaign.

In due course, after another visit to Philadelphia, Richard invited Sarah to Waterloo to meet his relations and to visit her possible future home. As was only proper, Mary Ann and I were invited as well, as it would have been indecent under the circumstances for a young woman to travel alone.

Accordingly, we made something of a holiday of it to journey up the canal with Sarah to Waterloo, New York, and taking a side trip to see the great falls at Niagara. While I had traveled previously to the Empire State, our journey to Waterloo and beyond was the farthest west I had ever been in my life. In some ways I was reminded of my initial foray to Philadelphia and the strange feelings that can arise when one ventures off in new directions.

We found Waterloo to be a small, bustling community awash with both industry and a small meeting of Hicksite Quakers. It was also evident that, in addition to being a gentleman, Richard was very successful and prominent within the local community. It was a pleasant sojourn with mixed feelings as we recognized that it might result in Sarah moving away from us to a new world. At the time we viewed it as a potential home for our niece. Little did we know that it shortly would become our home for the next twenty years.

As we departed from Waterloo after our visit, Richard let it be known to me, in a most appropriate manner, that he had asked for Sarah's hand and she had accepted. This did not surprise me, as there was obvious affection between the two, but it opened up new vistas of confusion for me as the girl's guardian. Clearly I had to, and did, consult with Mary Ann forthwith. After a short discussion, we agreed to the pending nuptials and subsequently Sarah and Richard were wed in 1837. While we regretted that the wedding would mean disownment for Sarah and her loss from our home, we found Richard to be eminently agreeable and a fine man. We shared many commitments and causes and I grew, over the years, to value his counsel on many matters. He had a practical bent that was of great benefit to me as I sometimes found my head lost in the clouds.

Sarah's marriage soon caused us to take another turn on the road of life. Her decision to move west to join in matrimony with Richard caused us to take action. On several occasions we journeyed out to Waterloo just as Richard continued his visits to Philadelphia. On one of those occasions, probably the one after Richard asked Sarah for her hand, Richard broached the idea of our family settling in the Waterloo area. He was well aware that business conditions were not exemplary in Philadelphia, and he believed there was opportunity in Waterloo. And so there was. As soon as I indicated some interest in this, Richard introduced me to Samuel Lundy, who ran an existing apothecary shop in Waterloo and who Richard believed might be interested in selling his shop. This indeed turned out to be the case.

Given that Samuel was also related to Benjamin Lundy and knew of my association with him, we were quickly able to reach a satisfactory agreement that I could afford and one that would offer us a successful establishment to move into. Richard made his own overture to solidifying the move by offering us the rental of one his houses at very favorable terms. In rapid order we reached agreement on all matters and set in motion the necessary actions to remove ourselves to Waterloo.

The family all had mixed feelings about this event, but the die was cast and we were off to a new adventure. We would leave Philadelphia with much regret, but the timing and circumstances were right. Personally, while I had my fears, I rejoiced that our family would remain as one. Accordingly we made plans to remove to Waterloo in 1836 so that we could become settled and Sarah could enjoy more of Richard's companionship prior to their marriage.

***

The Memories of Thomas M'Clintock

EMP. I believe my father's comment about wealth comes from my sister Mary and me. When we were younger and more impressionable, we did note the differences between ourselves and such people as the Hunts; amid our musings we probably did make some unfortunate comments about our parents' relative lack of wealth or our desire for it. In retrospect, I regret these comments. My parents always provided amply for our needs, supported us with funds when we engaged in various ventures, and certainly provided the necessities of life for us. I know now, from a distance of years, that money was simply not the priority for my parents. Indeed, by many standards they had more than adequate wealth but never made an issue of it. They had callings that were far greater than money for them and, in the end, more important than any financial concerns.

As is evident in my father's writings, my parents must have worried about money at various times in their lives. My sisters, brother, and I never heard these concerns nor were caused to fret about them. I take it as a matter of great honor that I was able to ease any concerns they might have had about finances in their later years by providing for them.

My father writes rather blithely about the most traumatic event of my youth. While he is correct in indicating that all resolved itself in a satisfactory manner, it was a monumental upheaval. Almost overnight, or so it seemed, I was to be uprooted from everything and everyone I had ever known.

Other than my sisters, Sarah was the most intimate friend I had to that point. Her entry into our home, while marked by a sad event, was a blessing to me that I will always cherish. She was a delight and, in many ways, the older sister I did not have. We were close enough in age that we had always shared a seemingly special bond, and that bond only deepened upon her entry into our family sphere. I could confide in her, expose my secrets to her, and learn the ways of young womanhood from her.

To Waterloo

I confess that the thought of another person taking her away from me was deeply upsetting. So while the move to Waterloo resolved the dilemma of distance, I was deeply affected by Richard's wooing and the attention he lavished on her. I have had little interaction with the emotion of jealousy in my life, but I suspect that is what I was undergoing at the time. Initially I was not very pleasant to Richard, although we grew to be friends over the years. I thought him very old and, indeed, he was more the age of my father than Sarah's own age. To be blunt, I thought his attentions scandalous and highly inappropriate. I know it was the manner of the time for a widower to seek to remarry soon after the death of a wife, but I was aghast nevertheless. It was not my place to say so but I am sure my actions and moods reflected my opinion.

But my opinion did not hold sway, even though I had expressed it to Sarah, and it became clear that Richard and Sarah were going to wed. She made it abundantly apparent to me, in no uncertain terms, that she cared for Richard and did not choose to live out her life as a spinster. In short, although I was not told so in so many words, her decision to marry was none of my business and I could do very well to take my fifteen-year-old nose and poke it elsewhere. This decision I grew to accept with greater age and maturity, but it was awfully painful to me at the time.

What was worse in my eyes was the decision to move to the frontier, for that is how I viewed Waterloo. While my parents saw a chance for a new beginning, I envisioned only a small town, remote for all else and off in the wilds, that was decidedly not Philadelphia. Bearing in mind that I was young at the time, this move very distinctly did not meet with my approval. I was expected to take my leave from my friends, my extended family, and all the joys that Philadelphia held in exchange for a modest town in which people actually kept cows in their yards—I thought not! It was to me like going to the very ends of the earth where Indians roamed freely.

Who knew what horrors awaited us or what privations we would suffer in such an uncivilized land. Naively, I was appalled that we would even consider such a life-changing move. I considered my parents most insensitive to the needs and concerns of their children, especially the needs and concerns of their daughter Elizabeth.

The roads were unpaved, the houses were clapboard, cows and other farm animals appeared to graze freely, and the people were crude and unsophisticated. And while my own dress was plain, it was clear that they placed little emphasis on the latest fashion or, in some cases, simple cleanliness. While my viewpoint changed over the years, I had very definite opinions and beliefs. Such were the complaints I enumerated to my parents along with many tears and copious weeping. Even though I had visited Waterloo on several different dates, it held no charms for me.

But my complaints did not sway the day. On this both my father and mother held firm, and it was one of the few times in my memory that they held to their position in the wake of numerous laments from their children, for they really were kind and caring souls.

While it would take some months to prepare, we were off to New York, Waterloo, and other terrors that awaited us. Just as Napoleon had his Waterloo, so I had mine.

Chapter Seven
Waterloo

As I hearken back to the twenty years we spent in Waterloo, it seems that much that occurred during those times has already passed into myth and legend. Consequently, I would spend some time on those days. But I get ahead of myself, for first we had to get there.

Deciding to locate to Waterloo was, in some ways, easier than getting there. Other than our transition to the north of Philadelphia, we had no experience in moving a household, and that earlier move did not require moving a business as well. As was our wont, Mary Ann and I prepared a list of all the myriad activities that needed to be accomplished. Little did we know as we compiled our list how many more tasks would need our attention.

Early on we determined that our actual relocation would best be completed in the late spring or early summer to allow the canal to be open so we might become established in our new home in time for the upcoming school year. Accordingly, we made our plans with that schedule in mind. To us, there were four major tasks which needed to be completed: transporting our household goods, hopefully selling my emporium and hauling my inventory of goods, transferring our Meeting membership, and saying our good-byes to friends and associates. Out of ignorance we paid little attention to what would be needed at the other end, and we suffered from that oversight upon our arrival.

Fortunately for me—for this was my greatest worry as we needed the funds to complete the transaction with Samuel Lundy—I was able to sell my business at some profit to a previous apprentice, Thomas Husband, who wished to take over an existing establishment and, more importantly, the existing clientele. I was able to accomplish this goal early on, which in turn allowed for an orderly transition to the new owner. Through the recommendation of others, I was then able to find teamsters and their like who would arrange for the crating and shipping of my inventory. This was of great concern to me as I had much of my funds tied up in my inventory and glassware. Having that material intact in Waterloo was critical to my future success. Luckily, I engaged a trustworthy firm and my fretting about my supplies turned out to be needless.

Likewise, our household goods, beds, tables, clock, etcetera, were packed up by the same firm. Needless to say, we were exceeding nervous about putting all our eggs in one basket, as they say. It is a tribute to Mary Ann's fine hand and oversight that all was done to our satisfaction, and to our immense relief, all arrived both on time and in one piece.

The only other major task was obtaining a minute from our Meeting to transfer to Junius in Waterloo. As expected, this was easily accomplished. I was honored during this process by being recognized as a minister from my Meeting and likewise obtaining a minute to that effect.

***

EMP. While my father was clearly moved by this recognition as a minister, like many things he makes light of it in his writing. To be acclaimed by the Hicksite Friends as a minister speaks loudly to the truths he imparted and the satisfaction with which they were received. This was not always the case, as at various times he was referred to as a ranter and at some Quaker Meetings was treated with a great deal of disrespect, particularly among various Meetings in New York City.

Personally, I always found his words soothing and full of calm wisdom. When I was younger, I simply noted when my father ministered and I found his words reassuring regardless of the message, for he spoke in measured tones with an almost biblical cadence. As I grew older, I came to appreciate the messages he imparted and the depth behind each remark. While there were often others who disagreed with his words, I always perceived him to be logical, evenhanded, and capable of humor when the moment called for it.

***

Saying good-bye to dear friends was much more difficult than I anticipated. I do not shed tears easily, but these good-byes were a time of remorse for me. I did not know what the future would bring in terms of connections with friends. Moving West meant a journey of days or weeks, depending on the mode of transportation, and I doubted many would ever make that arduous trek. I shared numerous embraces with those I might never see again and in some cases, due to age, I was sure I would not. It was agony for me.

Realizing that I might not see George again reaped the worst pain of my life, other than the mournful death of Julia. Yet as events would have it, my brother in spirit would remain a steady friend into my future. There is not a day that has gone by in recent years that I do not bless the advent of the rail system and the ease of transport that it provides. But at the time of our departure, I could not anticipate any of that progress, and parting felt like a final step.

And so we left Philadelphia.

We made our way to Waterloo in the accustomed manner of the time- journeying by boat as far as possible through New York City, up the Hudson, further making our way by canal to our final destination. In all, with various stops, the trip took almost three weeks. While we had made the trip on several occasions before, suffering through vile food and the coarse boatmen, this was the first time the trek included all the children and Sarah.

Having Charlie and Julia with us provided moments of great humor but, for the most part, we were variously occupied with keeping the children out of mischief, away from the danger of the countless bridges, and in avoidance of boredom. While many have ventured on such a trip, if I had my choice I would not do it again. One can only make so many comments about the slowly passing scenery to occupy young minds. We did have some parts of an early Dickens work for amusement, but that did not hold the interest of all concerned. Lizzie and Maggie were a great help with the younger children, but overall it was a trial for all, and arriving at our new home brought great relief.

***

EMP. Father's description of the parting from Philadelphia is consistent with my memory of those events. It was painful to all to depart from friends and companions whom we had known for our entire lives. Just as he had to say goodbye to dear friends, so did I. For my part, I felt as if I was being exiled to the remote outreaches of our country and I had little hope that I would ever see Philadelphia or my childhood friends again.

Regarding his description of our trip to Waterloo, I would differ on two counts. First, as I remember it, he was much different during our journey. A quiet man to begin with, he seemed to sink into a melancholy that I did not recognize with each day that the distance widened between us and Philadelphia. While he soon recovered from this state and regained his usual good humor shortly after our arrival in Waterloo, it marked the first of several states of melancholy I have noted in him during his life—each of short duration and all seemingly connected to some loss. I was unaware of the import he placed on his friends at the time, as I was suffering the loss of my own companions also and, as is typical of young girls of my age, my world was small and I stood at the center of it. I know now that he had suffered the loss of his family when quite young and I surmise that this had had a great influence on him.

Likewise, Father makes light of the exceedingly slow journey north and west. Perhaps I have been spoiled in the intervening years by the speed of rail transport, but I remember the trip as interminable. Three weeks of living on a various boats was almost more than I could bear. In particular, each day passed woefully slowly while we were confined on the small packet boat that plied the canal. There was little to do but gaze at the passing scenery, which chiefly consisted of trees, farms, and the occasional rude village.

While father took some delight in the richness of the land and farms, undoubtedly due to his upbringing on one, it seemed to me that New York consisted largely of vast fields of wheat and slow moving cows. Every tedious mile served to remind me of the different world we were moving to and how much I suspected I would not like it. In addition to my father's melancholy, I probably brought my own, but my parents made little note of it or simply chose to ignore it. I know not which.

***

In the end, we arrived safely in Waterloo, staying with Richard for several weeks until our belongings caught up with us. His hospitality, while beneficial to him as it allowed him further congress with Sarah, was most welcome to the rest of us as it allowed us some measure of repose. This was the most ease we would have for some time, as there was little to do without our belongings and my supplies. We busied ourselves by becoming more familiar with our new community and meeting diverse people who resided there.

It was an immense boon that Richard was well respected in the town, and many doors opened to us that might have otherwise remained shut. We made our first visits to Junius and found it a congenial Meeting. From the first, it was apparent that the Meeting contained like-minded souls much committed to reform, although it appeared that their commitment to the abolition cause was casual at best. Waterloo did not seem to be much affected by the strife over slavery. While it would take some time, Mary Ann and I resolved to rectify that matter with all haste.

After the wait of some weeks, our belongings did catch up at last. This sent us into a bustle of activity as we needed to thoroughly clean and prepare the inside of our new home, arrange furniture, and complete all such endeavors that come with setting up a new home. I confess that much of the burden of this tedious job fell to Mary Ann and the girls, as I was occupied with all that was required to establish my new apothecary shop.

This turned out to be a more time-consuming task than I had originally expected. Certainly I had started a new business before and had moved to a new locale, so I had some experience in this matter. What I had never faced before was building a steady stream of customers among complete strangers in an unfamiliar town. This proved to be an extremely rigorous and complex undertaking. Many were the long nights I laid awake contemplating the lack of clientele and the drain that placed on our set-aside funds.

Cleaning shelves and stocking them with supplies to my satisfaction proved to be the simplest of the tasks before me. In short order, I had the store prepared to receive customers. But where to find patrons proved to be a problem of another nature. While Samuel Lundy had done much to smooth the way for me, I was still a stranger to the new town. And, like many small villages, or so I have been told, they did not easily cozy up to strange faces, let alone entrust their business and health to them. It probably did not help that, true to my beliefs, I made much of the store being an emporium that would not dispense or sell products made from slave labor. To my knowledge, mine was the first such establishment in town with that mark, and that decision may have had some effect on potential patrons who viewed me as an agitator from the East. Likewise, I did not know the local physicians, nor did they know my work, so they were not an initial source of customers.

By my standards it was exceedingly slow process to build my business. Fortunately for us, we had funds to fall back on from the sale of my business in Philadelphia and some monies that Mary Ann had inherited from the sale of John Wilson's land grant in Ohio. These monies, along with generous terms from Samuel Lundy and Richard, tided us over, but there were many times in the first several years that I questioned our decision to remove ourselves to Waterloo.

I was, I confess, naïve about what it meant to live in a small village. In Philadelphia I was accustomed to the largeness of scale and the vast population. One's social circle in Waterloo, however, was meager by the standards of the city, and what positive endorsement one shared with another had limited distribution. I was also used to being in a city in which Quakers were large in number. That was not the case in Waterloo. Although a vocal group, we were a distinctly smaller sect than the other religious entities residing there. On a daily basis one rubbed elbows with others from various faiths, which were again different from Philadelphia where most of my encounters were with fellow Quakers. In the main I judged this to be a boon to me as I learned from the other faiths, but at the outset the babble of multiple faiths seemed to be a hindrance to my commercial ventures.

In Waterloo, it seemed that every utterance one made was repeated by another, and if one spoke to an individual, it seemed as if you were speaking to the whole village. Countless times I heard a person comment to me about something I had allegedly said or repeat some wild variation of a comment I had made in passing. All too often I would be accosted by someone challenging me on something I allegedly said, when in truth I had not made the utterance in the first place.

To be sure, I did not let the ignorance of others go unnoticed and remarked freely on state of affairs, but I hoped my comments were given some credence and sparked a spirit of free debate. But this was not always the case. Over time I grew to both accept this and to make use of it as I soon realized that if I said the correct thing to one person, it would spread to far more. It was most irritating at first. Many were the times when someone whom I assumed to be a potential customer entered my store only to find out they came to refute some comment I had supposedly made. To my great pleasure, I was able to turn some of these individuals into customers, but it took much time and the establishment of personal relationships. I found that I would have to build a clientele one person at a time.

While I have long held to the belief that people are the same the world over, the folk of Waterloo were different in some significant ways from what I had known before. Where those citizens of Philadelphia were marked by a politeness that often hid underlying insult, the people of Waterloo had directness and bluntness that made it abundantly clear when they disagreed with you. Likewise, there was no doubting whether or not you had been insulted. It was not my nature to take offense at much that is said by others, but there were words said on occasion that tried my patience, particularly those that disparaged the slave or Negro.

Much of this was probably of my own making. When we moved to Waterloo, I had resolved to speak out on the issues that concerned me, and I had little awareness of how that might be received in a smaller community. As I look back, I was probably overly expressive of my opinions at the outset, which was to my detriment. My own limited experience gave me much appreciation for that band of anti-slavery orators who traveled to towns espousing strong messages to utter strangers. I knew how hard their lot was, enduring difficult miles only to be met by the vilest of comments and derision. I often thought how lonely that profession must be for, in truth, with the exception of a small group in Waterloo, I was lonely as well.

Eventually conditions changed for the better as we survived the panic of 1837 and I made progress with the locals. Much effort went into placing advertisements in the local papers, making connections with neighboring physicians, supporting others engaged in commerce in the community, and, above all, remembering the lessons I had learned from Moses Bertram as to how to deal with one's clientele. It was a slow person-by-person endeavor, but it did ultimately reap results.

***

EMP. This is by far the most I ever heard from my father either about financial concerns or the trials of establishing oneself in a new town. He spoke of none of this to me or the other children. I assume he confided in my mother on these matters, as they discussed all things, but I cannot make that statement from any firsthand knowledge. My father was used to having a wide circle of friends who would converse with him frequently. This experience must have been hard on him as those he would number as friends were quite few. Added to this was the distance he felt from his friends in Philadelphia and I am sure the first few years in Waterloo were a trial to him.

It was different for us not to have Father's business connected to our home as we had on most previous occasions. While his store was close by and we were in and out of it frequently, there was a much greater sense that it was a separate sphere—one somehow separated from our daily lives. This is much more the normal state of commerce now, but at the time it was typical to have one's business in their home or for the family to reside above the store. Home and work were much the same back then.

For the rest of us the move turned out to be easier. Not having obligations at the store and with no school, we had freer rein to explore our new home and make acquaintances. Roaming through Waterloo took little time and there was little danger that any of us would lose our way, so we were given ample freedom.

The fields and waterways around the village proved to be of much interest to all of us and countless idle days were spent wandering aimlessly to see new sights. I found much to like about the town and my own fears regarding our move quickly subsided. In a similar fashion we could wander in and out of the stores in town and engage in various expeditions to obtain food and other needed victuals, all of which allowed us to both meet the people of the town and feel at ease there. I have always thought that moves such as ours must be easier for children than for adults, or at least that has been my experience. We had fewer fears and less to worry us, which made life easier by far.

In a similar fashion we began to make friends of our own age. Those whom we met in our various excursions seemed to welcome us. There was, I suspect, a curiosity on their part about the new people from the East. They would often question us about various aspects of living in a big city and contrast that with either what Waterloo had to offer or its lack thereof. I found the young people and the children to be most friendly and open. Oh, there were those who were rougher or in some cases cruder, but they were well-intentioned and honest. While we heard the occasional disparaging comment based on my father's views, they were of no major import to any of us.

We never encountered any negative reactions from any of the local citizens until we began venturing out on various petition campaigns. My father speaks more about this later, so I will defer any comment.

***

As our fortunes improved, so did life in Waterloo. Over time we made acquaintances and settled into something of a routine. The center of our lives was Junius Meeting. While a small Meeting, we found much contentment there. With the passing of years, the Meeting became more active in those causes that gave us satisfaction, as it became something of a hotbed of reform in our area. Likewise, our connections there led us to an active role in the Quarterly and Yearly Meetings as well. We found many kindred spirits through our association with the Yearly Meeting and especially with the Posts from Rochester. Isaac Post and I shared the same profession as druggists, and Amy and Mary Ann got along well together. In later years we shared with them an interest in the spirit world as well. They broadened our circle beyond the confines of Waterloo and gave us privy to others of a like mind in Rochester. I often regretted that they were distant in miles from us and our congress was limited.

All was not serious reform and the doings of the various Meetings with which we were associated, although I shall speak more about that at a later point. Our house became something of a social center, not only because we had eligible young women in our home who had suitors, but because we quickly found that Waterloo was not at the far ends of the earth, as far as visitors were concerned. Not only did we frequently entertain those who were on the reform circuit, but we also found that our friends had not forgotten us, nor did they think that a trip to Waterloo was without pleasure. Most who journeyed out to see us would also make a circuit to see other friends and family in the area, or they would take time to view the falls at Niagara as well. The Motts in particular made frequent trips to the area as Lucretia's sister, Martha, lived in nearby Auburn.

To my great pleasure, George, Catherine, and their brood also made the journey on several occasions. This, combined with our trips to Philadelphia and New York plus frequent letters, served to keep us in touch with our long-time friends. It was always my intent to return to Philadelphia, but in the meantime we maintained contact with those who were dear to us. It helped Mary Ann and the rest of the family knowing that George and Margaret Pryor were nearby, and we saw them often in our home and theirs.

That is not to say that all occasions were pleasant in our early years in Waterloo. While much of the discord seemed to center on my store, all of the family encountered challenges at various times. We resolved to keep a calm demeanor throughout those adversarial meetings, but at times it was not easy. One can only be accosted in the streets so many times before the challenge of confronting an adversary begins to wane, but those occasions became fewer and fewer over the years.

***

EMP. On this last point I disagree with my father. While my mother, sister, and I received the rare comment when soliciting signatures during the petition drives, we were never accosted in any inappropriate way or subjected to needless harassment. I suspect his comment is more a reflection of the negative image others had of my father when we first arrived in Waterloo.

***

The children occupied themselves with school or friends, and books were a boon companion to all of us. Reading to oneself and aloud to others became our most frequent form of entertainment. Many a night we would crowd around the fireplace before bed with an engaging tale, reading aloud to the entire family. As the eldest, Lizzie would most often take the lead in this pastime and I found her voice both soothing and entertaining. She had an ability to speak in the voices of various characters that we all found extremely amusing. As we had young children in the house, not all of the reading was necessarily of my liking, as the children seemed to most appreciate stories that would entertain and amuse them. My own tastes ran to more serious works of a religious and philosophical nature, but my youngsters had little patience for these.

During the long winter months, we would gradually work our way through various works, reading a chapter each week or a few pages every day. In this way, we read the works of Dickens, Hawthorne, and Stowe, just to name a few that I can remember. To that end, I can still recall with great delight the joy that the children would demonstrate when I returned home from travels with new books from their favorite authors.

I used this experience with books, coupled with a few other creative ideas, to expand some of the opportunities in my store. As most of the family enjoyed corresponding with others and we all read with great passion, I deemed that others might partake of those activities as well. As a consequence, I expanded my line beyond the apothecary business to include the sale of stationary, writing supplies, and, most of all, books and periodicals. While I ensured there was an ample supply of materials of a reform nature—selling *The Liberator*, and carrying the works of authors such as the Grimkes, Parker, Douglass, and others—I confess that the briskest traffic was in the narrative work of the day and the various periodicals that appealed to women and those individuals conscious of fashion. For the most part, I left this area to Lizzie to manage as I had little interest in it except for the books that attracted me. She was excellent at this task and very soon the bookstore portion of my establishment was turning a tidy profit. Not only did books become a valuable part of the store, but they brought new customers into the apothecary who might not otherwise have darkened our door.

As I reread the previous pages, it would appear that we were quite serious and that I directed most of my energy to the making of a profit. To the latter, I confess there is a great deal of truth as I was much concerned with our success in the early years. To the former, that does not jibe with my memory. It has always seemed to me that the children had a great deal of fun and merriment, of which Mary Ann and I could partake in. During the summer we tended to our garden, and we all greatly enjoyed the strawberries we grew there. In the winter, the children would skate on the frozen canal, and we all took pleasure in long sleigh rides, while nested under blankets, over the country roads.

The winters, even with their various frozen activities, I did not enjoy. Waterloo seemed to me to be much colder and the winters far longer than my native Philadelphia. There were months at a time where it felt as if I could not shake the cold from my bones. At times, I would find myself envious of the food that we cooked as I knew that it, at least, was warm. As long as we lived there, I did not become accustomed to the wind, cold, and snow of the winters. Similarly, the winters seemed to isolate us from the outside world. Until the time that rail travel became reliable, it was as if a cocoon of snow and ice descended upon us and removed us from the world at large. When we at last left those cold months behind, I held no regret.

For entertainment, all was not just reading. On occasion we would sing together as I still maintained my love of music; even though the Quakers did not make music a central part of worship, I still found it able to stir great emotions in me. I was not exalted for my own musical talents; indeed, I was usually asked to refrain from all but listening, but all of the women could carry a tune and I found it quite pleasant to listen to them harmonize. I would purchase the music of the Hutchinsons as frequently as I was able and found that Mary Ann and the girls could make much of their tunes.

Likewise, for a period of time we amused ourselves with explorations into the world of spirits. Through the Posts, we had become exposed to the rappings of the Fox sisters and the attendant hullabaloo. I regret what became of the sisters and their descent into a theatrical showpiece, as I found much of what they explored of great interest. The notion that we could communicate with those on the other side was congenial with my beliefs, and we spent many hours exploring that realm. I, myself, had little skill or talent in that area, but there were nights that we and others spent huddled around our parlor table asking questions and seeking answers in taps and other signs. We had little luck with this matter, so I still have questions in my mind regarding the veracity of the subject and the claims of contact made by others.

With mesmerism we had greater success. Lizzie appeared to have a rare talent for this endeavor and would allow herself to be put into a trance to explore the spirit world. On occasion she would speak in the voice of someone departed but unfortunately never delivered any great insight. She had some reluctance to do this as her brother would often try, sometimes successfully, to engage her in silly acts while she was in her trance state. As he was the most successful in assisting her to achieve this state, he would also make suggestions to her that the rest of us found unseemly, although often humorous.

To this day, I do not know the truth of the spirit world as there were many charges of fraud around it and we had little success with it. But we spent many an hour making the attempt and in speculation about it. At the least it helped to pass some of the long winter nights.

Over time, we settled into the routine of life. My business grew able to provide for the needs of all, the schooling was satisfactory for the children, we all made friends whom we cherished, and Waterloo became our home. While we knew we would leave it at some point in time, it embraced us.

***

EMP. It is odd how memories vary of similar experiences. I remember our winters in Waterloo as times of great joy, perhaps due to my greater freedom to explore and participate in the wonders the frozen land could create. My father speaks of skating and sleigh rides, and I, too, remember those moments fondly. But there was much more to the winter months. I remember the ice glistening in the sun, the beauty of the moon and stars on bright nights, and the sense of warmth that would envelope you when you came into a building or house after dashing through the cold. It was the best time of the year for me, perhaps because I could use the clothes I wore to stay warm where in the summer my clothing only seemed to make the heat that much more unbearable.

I, and I think the other children, also remember the times reading together with great fondness. There is a sense of being together that reading aloud to one another seems to bring. In many ways, it was akin to being in Meeting on those occasions when you feel as one with others who are present with you. There was nothing religious about our reading together, but it was special to all of us nonetheless. Father speaks accurately as well about our excitement when he would return home with a new book. While we looked forward to his stories about his travels and adventures, secretly we waited for the unveiling of the newest tome he had purchased in his travels. The works of Dickens, in particular, captivated us all, and we could look forward to spending many pleasurable nights engrossed in his latest.

My mother and father did not let reading become simply a pleasure, however. They expected that we would engage in vigorous discussions of the merits of the work we were reading, debate freely the ideas expressed in the book, and, above all, formulate an opinion. I can well remember poor little Julia being asked her opinion when she was no more than six or seven. Often she struggled valiantly just to stay awake, and to be asked to think as well proved difficult for the young girl. Certainly my parents recognized this, but they would ask regardless.

Charlie was a different matter as he always saw the humor in any situation no matter how grim the subject. This, my parents found exasperating but in the end came to regard it as his nature. My sister and I often watched this with greatly disguised glee as my parents would end a conversation with Charlie by commenting that "thee are being ridiculous." We all recognized this as a sign not to go further and even Charlie would desist at his point, even though they always made that comment with small smiles of amusement.

I blush now when I think of our experiments with contacting the spirits and mesmerism. Through the years I followed the exploits of the Fox sisters and others, and I now believe them to be noncredible. I think that they acted in such a way as to draw attention to themselves, rather than for truth, and others were able to capitalize on this. My parents and others who explored this phenomenon were motivated by a search for the truth, which may also explain their lack of success in reaching that goal. Of Mesmer's process I am less certain. Certainly when I was a subject of these "spells," I felt and behaved differently. Often times, as well, I had little memory of what had occurred. However, I do not believe the process involved spirits in any way. Rather, it was and is some other form of consciousness. Regardless, I left these practices behind when we left Waterloo and have not been inclined to seek them out again.

Photographs

Thomas M'Clintock

Mary Ann Wilson M'Clintock

Mary Ann M'Clintock Truman

James Truman

Waterloo

Burroughs Phillips

George Truman

Catherine M. Truman

The Memories of Thomas M'Clintock

Jane Hunt

Richard Hunt

Lucretia Mott

James Mott

Chapter Eight
Reform

Outside of the welter of family activities and my trade, it is difficult to look back and sort out all that occurred during our twenty years in Waterloo. Indeed, there were times when we had to restrain ourselves or the numerous reform activities we were engaged in, or they would have swallowed up all of our time and energy. Even as I recollect those days, it is difficult to shift through all we were committed to and participated in. In remembering, I have chosen to put my attention to those activities that seemed central to me, those that spoke the loudest to me. I shall speak briefly of those other areas but not dwell on them to any great extent.

When we removed ourselves to Waterloo, Mary Ann and I resolved that we would speak out on our views in all forums. This we did, in countless different ways and to numerous audiences, although primarily within the broad Hicksite community. It was our belief that failure to act on our beliefs was one of the greatest sins we could face. While this caused us some disruption initially upon our arrival in Waterloo, we found kindred spirits soon enough.

We were greatly aided in our efforts by the support of our children, particularly Elizabeth and Mary Ann. The younger children provided more of their support through their acceptance of us being gone from our home, or by their cooperation when asked to sleep on the floor when we had guests, which was often. Lizzie and Maggie often accompanied us on our rounds or took independent action of their own making. I have always been proud of my children, even when their path differed from mine.

***

EMP. While I was in agreement with my parents on almost all of their activities, there was no doubt about what was expected of us. Just as other young people had chores around the home or farm, so were we expected to be out striving for reform and advancement. I often compared our actions to those we knew who were required to witness for their religious faith and, in doing so, convert others to their way of thinking. Ours was not religious exhortation, but we were expected, almost mandated, to bear witness, for our parents strongly believed that actions spoke louder than idle words. Words without action were seen by them as meaningless. On this I agree, as I have often been struck by the hypocrisy of those who advocate for one thing and behave in an altogether different manner. Yet there were times when it was a trial to abide by my parents' wishes, as there were often other social activities I wished to engage in.

Even though Sarah and Julia received initial dispensation when they were younger, they too were soon enlisted in the Waterloo army of reform. Only Charlie seemed to be able to shirk this duty. Why I have never been sure, but he was clearly not held to the same standard as my sisters and me. Somehow he was able to avoid these tasks through combination of his sense of humor and, dare I say it, the fact that he was a male.

***

It goes without saying, although I shall speak more of this later, that we were ably supported in all manner of reform, including abo-

Reform

lition, by our friends and colleagues at Junius Meeting. While we were initially fearful that they were not allies in the fight against slavery, we soon found that their spirits were true to the cause and of much assistance. In later years we counted on our friends at Junius to be in attendance in mass for meetings on all manner of reforms. Whether they verbalized their positions or not, their presence spoke out.

Of the reforms we engaged in, four took predominance: the antislavery doings we had begun in Philadelphia, temperance, religious freedom, and the rights of women. Each of these we found consistent with our belief that God existed in all things and that the world could become a better place for all concerned if people but applied themselves in the proper direction and spoke the truth.

In other areas we applied ourselves, including the plight of the Indian, the turmoil in Europe, and the famine in Ireland, but they seemed but passing fancies in terms of our day-to-day actions. So, too, did we dabble in the efforts of various new reform communities, such as Skaneateles, but we did not seriously consider affiliating with such a place or moving to one, even though we provided what financial support that we could to help them. On this we found Margaret and George's ill-fated exploration to be a harbinger of the future of such places.

The tragedy of the Indians did occupy much of our time and effort. Their cause many at Junius had embraced prior to our arrival and we were in much support of their endeavors. With the exception of Penn's early dealings with the Indians, the country's treatment of the Indians and uncounted violations of treaties was shameful at best. We were resolved not to allow Jackson's malevolent abuse of the Cherokee to be expanded to those in our vicinity.

***

EMP. As a young woman, it seemed to me that everyone who came to our door, or every article my parents read, would enlist us in some new cause or endeavor. Just as the peddlers seemed to know at which door to knock for a sale, so it was with any itinerant reformer. He or occasionally she had only to rap at our door to receive entrance, a fair hearing, and oftentimes a meal and a bed. At times I found this immensely frustrating and confounding. How, I reasoned, could we truly make a difference when our energies were pulled in five or six seemingly different directions at once? Additionally it made the tasks of we children seem endless.

As I grew older, I realized that my parents were steadfast in their belief that the efforts of men and women could make our world better. That there was a true and just society that we should strive for at all times and against all odds seemed to be an eternal goal they strove to reach. While their approach was deeply rooted in their Quaker upbringing where mine was not, their striving was consistent and all pervasive.

***

Through these and other efforts we made the acquaintance of a wider range of reform-minded individuals ranging from Rochester to Syracuse. Through travel and meetings, we met those we admired, such as the Posts and Frederick Douglas in Rochester, and Samuel May in Syracuse. Each of these proved to be true companions in the fight for a just and fair society.

As I talk about companions, and there were many who shall be mentioned, I am struck by one chance encounter that has stayed with me due to events of the near past. During the time that either Mary Ann or Aunt Margaret or I accompanied Abby Kelley on her rounds as she stirred up ferment among the people, I was with her during one of her meetings when I chanced to notice one particular member of the audience. This of itself was of little note, for I often watched the audience as I had heard dear Abby speak on many occasions.

This gentleman was of some note, however, as he sat erectly, dead center in front of Abby and stared at her with great intensity. His gaze, in fact, was so powerful that it bordered on fierceness and seemed to contain portents of violence. Seldom have I seen another that invoked fear, but this man beheld that look. I remarked on this later to Abby with some concern, and she informed me that she knew the man, that he often attended her meetings, particularly in the northern part of the state, and meant her no harm. That man was John Brown.

To my knowledge, I never saw him again, but I have thought about that short encounter in light of the tragic events of Harpers Ferry. Perhaps I shared his passion and commitment on the slavery question, but I could not countenance his actions. While I mourn the man as a human being, I cannot hold with those that consider him a martyr to a glorious cause. Violence and the taking up of arms in the name of any cause are unjustified.

**

EMP. The above comment regarding John Brown I never heard from my father while he was alive. I thought I knew my parents well, but I am continually surprised by minor comments that he makes almost in passing that come to me as sweet insights. My father abhorred violence and slavery in equal measure, so Brown was an enigma for him. To the end of his days he was unsure as to how to judge him.

**

And so I move on to the events of the day and the activities that encompassed our enthusiasms for forty years and more.

Chapter Nine

Temperance

Of demon rum and its like, I have had little personal experience. Oh, in my travels I have partaken of the occasional small beer or sipped a glass of wine in celebration of some date or momentous event. But we never kept spirits in our home and, for the most part, we existed as a teetotaling household. There were certainly times in which it was difficult to avoid alcohol as it was abundant at so many events, but I believe my family and I were successful in large measure although I believe Charlie may have tempted fate as a young man on several occasions.

Of the evil of alcohol I have no doubt. The Quakers, as a body, have little tolerance for the use of spirits and other beverages containing alcohol, but there were certainly those who indulged to their detriment. Likewise, one could not live in a large city like Philadelphia without noting the numerous taverns and observing those who frequented such establishments. There were and are rowdy areas of that fair city that attracted a less than savory clientele intent on debauchery and licentiousness. Alcohol was ever present for those who marched to that tune. Even in the small environs of Waterloo and Seneca Falls there were those who would have been at home in the worst part of Philadelphia.

The Memories of Thomas M'Clintock

While in Philadelphia I could avoid the worst evils of alcohol, as those with whom we associated were temperate to the extreme. In Waterloo that was not the case. The perils of a small village in relation to a reformer existed in great abundance for those who consumed alcohol as well. It was noted and commented on when someone had overindulged in spirits or when the drink had caused an honest man to go astray. All noticed and remarked on the drunkard and sometimes that drunkard lived next door to you, for it was a small town. The merchants of the town, including myself, were often most aware of the evils of drink, for we were the ones the indigent or abused housewife came to for credit or, in my case, both credit and remedies for the effect of drink. Would I have been able to concoct a remedy for the effects of drink or, better yet, a potion that would prevent someone from drinking, I would have been wealthy beyond measure. I believed that anyone with an ounce of sense could easily see the link between drink and violence, theft, and countless other forms of immorality.

As a chemist the issue of temperance was something of a quandary for me. In my line of work, it was fairly easy to avoid the use of slave products as there were few products I would have sold in my store that were produced by slaves, with the exception of cotton dressings for wounds. Avoiding the use of alcohol was a far different matter, however.

In the first part, there were, and I suspect still are, many physicians who recommended a dose of alcohol for a variety of ills. There are those who make light of individuals who ingest alcohol for medicinal purposes, but at the time I was practicing, doctors believed that as well. While I am not a physician, George and I had vigorous discussions on numerous medical matters. As in many things, we were of like minds on the use of alcohol, laudanum, and bloodletting. All were common practices but ones that I saw little value in, other than having someone become excessively weak due to the

Temperance

loss of blood, indisposed due to the effect of the alcohol, and, more insidiously, obsessed with the properties of laudanum. While laudanum has many useful applications related to the alleviation of pain and suffering, it also encourages the continual use over extended periods of time. Both laudanum and alcohol seem to possess properties that are debilitating, and that can lead to the ruin of individuals and their families.

Even where I would wish to avoid the use of alcohol in remedies provided to our citizens, its use was most pervasive. Many, if not all, of the bottled remedies provided by others seemed to contain excessive dosages of alcohol as part of the basic mixture. Certainly, those who provided nostrums that purported to cure most of the ills that one could encounter contained substantial quantities of alcohol. I was always amazed at the number of teetotaling citizens who did not hesitate to ingest vast quantities of these substances when, at the same turn, they would refuse to partake of ardent spirits or any other drink of an alcoholic nature. In my store, I strove to sell products that contained more healthful properties based on vegetable products or herbal remedies, but it was impossible to completely avoid the sale of products containing alcohol, for among the supplies I stocked was alcohol, which I used in some of my preparations.

It is my belief that drink is the major cause of many of our ills of society, and Mary Ann and I resolved to do what we could to stamp out that scourge. As a consequence, we vigorously advocated for temperance in our communities. At various times, we posted broadsheets in the community, sponsored the touring speaker, and conducted meetings in the room above my store. In all that we did personally, we tried to be exemplars of temperance ourselves.

But, after long reflection, I confess that much of this was to little avail. Too often we found ourselves speaking to those of like mind, and they were not generally affected by the sin of consumption. Oh, we felt good about ourselves and our efforts, but we failed noticeably to affect the drunkard and change his ways. Where we could, we ministered to those with the affliction or provided assistance to the wives who had been neglected by a drunken husband. But in the main, our efforts were futile. The only true success I ever saw was due the ministrations of those who had reformed themselves as the Washingtonians had done. These people seemed to have the power to persuade, but even they reached a sparse few.

Alcohol was one of the few things of the time that men and women shared equality in. While only women of the lowest nature frequented the taverns and saloons, it was clear to me in my practice that the abuse of alcohol was not confined to men. The number of women who consumed alcohol may have been fewer, but the effects did not draw boundary lines among the sexes.

I have preached against the evil of alcohol for many years and count my blessings that its reach has not extended to my family. But, I despair at truly eradicating it from our midst. For every church that is built, every school that is erected in hope, it seems that one or more taverns are also built. Without a permanent ban on the sale and production of alcohol, which is implausible, I fear the effects of the toxic substance will never leave our land. If I had my druthers I would eradicate it from the land, but I suspect the effects of the cure would be worse than the disease.

Of all my efforts and all the reforms I have engaged in, the fight against alcohol is one that I have failed in. I count it as a significant lack on my part and can only take consolation in the fact that others have failed as well.

***

EMP. There is a note of frustration with my father's comments on temperance that does not appear elsewhere. While he had his setbacks in other arenas, it is clear that he believed his efforts for temperance to be a failure. In this, he is not alone. I have had more

Temperance

experience and different years on earth and have seen countless others butt their heads against the scourge of alcohol. Many have marshaled forces against the peril and still it persists. Though it seems to me that the consumption of spirits and their pervasiveness in our lives has decreased, the effects remain.

Father also seems to imply that alcohol affects the male as an imbiber and the female because of the male's action under the influence. In my own experience there were certainly women who overindulged in alcohol, but their affliction could be hidden behind the curtains of their home. Until I read his comments, I never heard that he shared that view and had experienced it in his store.

It is a sad plight when one loses one's life to a vile substance.

Chapter Ten
Anti-Slavery

Of our anti-slavery efforts I will, I fear, speak at much greater length. Even though it took the stroke of a pen and the Great War that we have recently emerged from to stay this evil from our shores, and even as I have my own mixed thoughts regarding our efforts, it has been the principal battle of my life. This conflict has drained my life force, left me at many times despairing of my fellow man and providing little hope for the future, but it was the right fight to engage in. I have no doubt in my own mind that truth resided on our side. Our cause was just, our tactics were superior, and, in the end, through the death of many, our results were achieved. But at what cost is often a question I still find myself unable to answer.

Yes, the blight of slavery has been removed from our shores, but the baseness with which we treat our colored brethren remains a blemish on the land. Even today as we emerge from the aftermath of the war and the elimination of slavery, the treatment of Negroes by many remains detestable. For many, anti-slavery failed to include equal rights as citizens for the Negro. Many, and I found this position illogical, could advocate for the abolition of slavery on one hand and on the other deny the rights of citizenship to a race of human beings.

The Memories of Thomas M'Clintock

As I have noted elsewhere, Mary Ann and I joined the fray with all our strength when we arrived in Waterloo. While my store and its free produce notation served as an opening salvo, there were countless other venues and avenues that we pursued as well, so many that it is difficult to know where to begin. But I shall try to bring coherence to what seemed to be a constant state of affairs, as it all seems to run together in an old man's mind. By the time we arrived in Waterloo, we had become closely affiliated with the AAS and its purposes and strategies. While acting independently, as did many, we were in accordance with their aims and beliefs.

In my memory, it seems that our first real action, which we had also been involved with in Philadelphia, was the petition campaign. The AAS had determined that one of the best ways to oppose slavery and to make our voices heard was to bombard Congress with petitions expressing our opinion of slavery on a variety of different levels. Whether it was general opposition to slavery or a more specific petition to abolish slavery in the District of Columbia, the AAS was to flood Congress with a call for action from the common man and woman. The AAS borrowed this strategy from our brethren in England, and we were in much support of it. This, along with the numerous anti-slavery speakers whom the AAS supported, was seen as both a way to raise the visibility of our cause and to hopefully attract new members as well.

We worked with the fury of demons to obtain signatures from citizens far and wide. In my store, I always had whatever petition we were currently endorsing on prominent display, and I discussed the merits of the sentiments with all who entered. As well, Mary Ann and the girls spent countless hours going from door to door within the village seeking support. If there was worth in the petitions, it is a tribute to their efforts, for they spent long hours trudging the streets and engaging all they encountered in conversation. To the immense credit of the worthy citizens of Waterloo, they met with great success. There was, of course, the occasional ruffian who made rude comments or disparaged their efforts. But they found nothing like the mobbing that others faced in the larger cities.

While they did not confine themselves solely to Waterloo and spread themselves out to Seneca Falls, Auburn, and other locations, Waterloo was well represented in the cascade we sent forth to Congress. If one could judge success and sway the day by the sheer weight and number of petitions we sent forth, then slavery would have been abolished in an instant.

But that was not to be. The response of Congress to our efforts was to invoke the infamous Gag Rule, as our representatives kowtowed to the cowardly efforts of the Southern slave owners, refusing to accept or acknowledge our pleas for freedom and the exercise of our rights as citizens. Even with the stalwart efforts of the esteemed John Quincy Adams, they could not see—or refused to see—the truth of what we said. While I have had little use for politics and politicians, and have consistently refused to become embroiled in that arena, I considered, and still consider, these actions in violation of the Constitution and the basic rights under English common law. In my readings of Blackstone, it would appear that the right of petition has been long held and respected by even the most autocratic king. I cannot understand how this basic right could be denied to citizens in a land that espouses itself as a bastion of liberty.

During these years I often despaired of our land and its citizens. I could not understand then, and cannot understand now, how a civilized nation could exist when it could not maintain civil discourse within its borders. Too often did I witness with my own eyes the violence of mobs exhorted by otherwise respectable members of society; too often did I hear curses and vile expressions hurled at those who disagreed. I despaired. Even the Quakers, that peaceable body, could be disruptive and impolite to those with whom they disagreed, as it was my misfortune to experience on several occasions.

The Memories of Thomas M'Clintock

***

EMP. I know of nowhere else to note it, but I am surprised that my father makes no mention of my trip to Philadelphia in 1838. In that year, my family honored me by sending me to attend the inaugural opening of the long-awaited Pennsylvania Hall, which was to be the bulwark of anti-slavery and free thought in Philadelphia. My parents had made what contribution they could to building the structure and were very supportive of all that it stood for. It was a singular honor for me that my parents allowed me to attend in their stead, as the demands of business and my mother's sometime precarious health precluded their attendance.

I traveled to and from that event with other companions who were making the same journey, so I was well shielded. Perhaps because I was almost giddy with excitement, the trip to Philadelphia and back did not seem as arduous as my previous jaunt up the canal. In any case, careful arrangements were made for my travel and stay in the great city. I received very detailed instructions from my parents regarding how to behave, what to wear, and how to present myself. As I had some concerns about the journey, myself being only seventeen, I found their comments reassuring and comforting.

In time, I made the journey arriving several days prior to the actual meeting so I could meet with friends and convey my parents' greetings to many. As well, there was some business I needed to conduct on behalf of my father with various houses that supplied to him. The first several days were both pleasant and successful; then came the actual gathering at Pennsylvania Hall. It was a grand hall and a tribute to the cause for which it stood.

I was thrilled to be there and to have the opportunity to hear Garrison, Grimke, Chapman, and Abby. It was by far the greatest collection of exalted voices that I would have the opportunity to hear in my lifetime. Looking back, I remember little of the speeches but much of the mob that surrounded the hall.

For two days we walked through hordes of ruffians and ne'er-do-wells as we made our way to the hall, constantly suffering from vile language and aspersions from an insufferable crowd of barbarians and slavers. I confess that I was terrified at times. It seemed that lawlessness had struck the city my family loved. Being jostled and pushed as I walked among a crowd was like nothing I had experienced before. While I had read about riots and mobs in the papers, to be in the midst of one was frightening beyond belief.

The inside of the hall was scarcely calmer. The din of the mob often rose over the speakers' voices, and one could constantly hear the push and growl of those outside. Added to the general din was the sound of windows breaking as stones and bricks were thrown through them. As well, the occasional blackguard was able to gain entry to the hall and they continually shouted at the speakers and showed all manner of disrespect. I shuddered to think what would become of this audience of men, women, whites, and blacks at the hands of the mob. Many of the speakers had dealt with these kinds of disruptions in the past and, for the most part, they were successful in retaining the attention of the audience so as to hear their message. In this Angelina Grimke was most effective and I was thoroughly impressed with her.

For two days we suffered abuse and degradation but continued with our deliberations on the issue of slavery against the impending violence from outside. On the third, as we continued the women's meeting of the Anti-slavery Convention, all escalated. At some point during the meeting, it was made clear to us by the mayor of Philadelphia that we must depart the premises of the hall. This, in turn was announced to the mob whose voices roused in a howled response. Into this maelstrom of mobsters, the white and colored women of the meeting would need to pass through. I foresaw it, ac-

curately I might add, as analogous to passing through an Indian gauntlet. I can still feel the fear that surrounded me on the part of all concerned as we contemplated the passage.

I shall never forget Lucretia at that movement. Without the appearance of a moment of thought, she announced that we would all depart arm in arm, one white woman with one colored woman. And so we did. Quietly we marched out past the crowd two by two and with our heads held high. Just the sight of the tiny Lucretia seemed to quiet the crowd, and we departed in a small semblance of peace.

The silence of our march out was offset by the violence that followed our departure. All too soon, that beautiful hall, that symbol of hope, was gone in flames. While hope for the movement burned in our hearts, our building was but a heap of ashes.

To my eternal regret, it soon followed that we, the abolitionists, were blamed by many for the violence and burning on the notion that we had somehow incited others due to the unsatisfactory nature of our thoughts and speeches. To this day I remain confused as to how people who raise their voices in peace against injustice can somehow be blamed for causing the violent actions of others. The logic of that stance escapes me and is incomprehensible. My stomach turned at this contempt, and for some time my thoughts turned away from Philadelphia.

***

To my friends and family I railed at this injustice, often casting strong messages against those that stood in our way. For a period of time we redoubled our efforts, sending even more petitions with more signatures on to the exalted Congress. But it was all for naught and in the end our work on voicing our views to Congress flickered out like a spent candle. While the candle of hope was relit at other times and with other attempts, it would show no more on the halls of Congress.

Anti-Slavery

That is not to say that the effort was futile, for in truth there was much good that came out of our failure. The largest good was the unfettering of our women members into the cause. The labors of women in the petition effort had been extreme, and the failure of those efforts only spurred them on to more action and exertion. While it had long been the practice among Quakers for women to have an equal voice, their sweat and struggle certainly earned them a commensurate place at the table among the males of the AAS. Rather than fading away in frustration, to their eternal credit the women redoubled their efforts in a multitude of ways—raising funds, speaking out against injustice, and maintaining their presence in the face of adversity.

***

EMP. The last comment by my father intrigues me. Both of my parents were deeply versed in women's literature of the time, having read Wollstonecraft and the Grimke sisters with their calls for the emancipation of women. Garrison as well spoke to the inequality that women faced to great effect. Likewise, both had been exposed to the hazards of women speaking to promiscuous audiences through their association with Abby Kelley and Lucretia. In short, they were well aware of the voices being raised about the treatment of women.

However, I find my father's thoughts insightful and prescient regarding future events. Here he equates the visibility of women within the anti-slavery movement to their actions. Clearly he believes that women achieved greater prominence through their labors in a sphere that was generally seen as belonging to men. Nowhere else have I seen someone make this connection, and while there were many forces at work regarding women, his insight bears noting. As he also cites elsewhere, the issue of women in the anti-slavery movement became a divisive factor.

***

The year 1840 seemed to mark a turning point in the movement, unfortunately around the issue of politics and women. All of our efforts to that time—the petitions, meetings, fund-raising, and expansion of our numbers—seemed to pale and be shunted aside for the new directions others advocated. To this time, the AAS had taken a position that the force of our moral arguments would ultimately win the day, and the slaves would be freed. Fundamentally, moral suasion was our strategy, although tactics to preach that message varied between speakers, pamphlets, free produce, and other measures designed to compel reflection if not deeds.

There were, however, those who disagreed and believed that the movement needed to embrace the political arena and create change through a legislative and elective course. They, including many prominent anti-slavery stalwarts, wished to work for the abolition of slavery through the elective process and the consequent legislation. From a perspective of intellect, I understood this view. The courts of the land and Congress had continued to grapple with the issue of slavery in the expanding Western territories, and our pleas for the abolition of slavery had fallen on deaf ears in that arena as witnessed by the Gag Rule and the Missouri Compromise. While I wished them well in their endeavors, I could not participate in that course of action as it was not in keeping with my beliefs as a Quaker. Many of those true to our cause, including Gerrit Smith and Henry Stanton, took that course and it weakened us considerably.

The desire for political action was, unfortunately, combined with the desire on the part of the AAS to bring women, in the person of Abby Kelley, into full participation as part of the leadership of the AAS. During our annual meeting Garrison brought these issues to the fore, knowing that he had the votes necessary to bring Abby onto the Board of Managers. As always, William was both astute

Anti-Slavery

politically (he had counted the votes prior to the meeting), and he was willing to push that which he believed to be right in the face of opposition. This resulted in a split of the AAS, with the political group striking out on their direction and those that remained loyal to Garrison staying with his leadership and direction. As ever, my family sided with Garrison.

***

EMP. My parents frequently asserted their loyalty to William, although this was not always easy and they did debate it at times. They loved him as a man and for the stands he took. However, like all men, he was not perfect and they knew this.

While my father wrote to the Liberator *in support of a number of William's more extreme stances on the Constitution and secession, they were much taken back by his hostility toward Frederick when he chose a different path away from Garrison. My father, in particular, never failed to disagree with someone when he felt they were in the wrong. He would not, however, attack their personal character, feeling that this was not a part of any argument and that nothing was served by it. Consequently, he was aghast at the vituperation William uttered on the pages of the* Liberator *against Frederick. While he held a steady course with Garrison throughout his life, his silence on the matter of Frederick spoke volumes. I was disappointed that he did not come out in support of Frederick, yet his refusal to defend William was striking in its own right.*

***

I have often pondered on my propensity for engagement in causes that result in divisions among people of like mind. During my life I have been intimately involved in several divisions among religious sides, seen the division of the anti-slavery forces, and sided with women in the cause of their emancipation. Each of these has resulted in the loss of friends, animosity among former colleagues, and lingering bitterness. I have never wondered about the truth of the side I chose, but have considered my willingness to stand for change when I risked the loss of friends. Is this willingness to forego friends, to cast them aside, some character flaw in myself? I grappled with this in the long hours spent on trains or coaches, as it concerned me greatly. That is probably for others to determine, but I know that each occasion brought me pain and grief.

Nonetheless, the now smaller band of Garrisonians marched forward. We would join the battle and continue on while holding true to our beliefs. As I have noted elsewhere, during this time I received encouragement from William to travel to the World Anti-slavery Congress in London, but lack of funds and the press of earning a living for my family precluded me from attending, although I was able to join with Richard in sending some wool cloth to William that was suitable for a new suit.

Garrison was constantly without funds, and I considered it a small miracle that he was able to secure the monies necessary for the trip. I envied him but took some consolation in the fact that he wore a suit that originated in Waterloo. As I understood it from those that attended, the Congress also split over the issue of women, and that division would eventually be rejoined in the future in Waterloo. I was greatly appreciative, as were the women in our family, that William ended on the side of the women, as I believe it was the right course of action.

It was shortly after the events of 1840 that I encountered the estimable Frederick Douglass for the first time. Douglass' history is well known by all, having escaped from slavery to become the foremost orator of the anti-slavery cause. As Douglass burst into the limelight, I was asked to accompany him on a speaking tour through the western parts of New York, as it was not deemed safe for him to travel alone as a colored man. I considered it an honor to be asked, but I had little concept of what I was inserting myself into. Fred was like a magnet that attracted all of the worst elements of our society—in particular those who chose to hate another simply due to the color of his skin.

Being with Frederick was the only time in my life that I truly felt fear and worry about my personal safety. There were few moments of real safety during our travels which occurred while in the home of some friend, or in the various churches and meeting places in which he spoke. This looming sense of danger had nothing to do with Frederick, who was delightful company and an earnest conversationalist. Rather, it had everything to do with the constant vilification, curses, jostling, and other forms of ill manners that he was subject to. I have little acquaintance with the emotion of hate other than from those days with him. Words cannot do justice to the violent expressions of distaste that countenanced the faces of many that we passed by. Not only did I fear for myself and Frederick during these times, but I likewise feared for the future of our country if this was what a man of color was expected to face.

I speak here largely of my own fears, for Frederick showed no outward sign of anger or discomfort. He was an imposing figure and, while an eloquent speaker who could raise others to tears, he showed no sign of recognition to the barbs of others. Oh, he would lash out and give vent in his many speeches, but to those who cast aspersions constantly upon him, he gave no sign that he heard them nor did he reply. Never have I seen such courage in the face of such hostility. I was humbled and relied more on him for my safety than I did to protect him. I was happy to survive these travails, and even more pleased to consider Frederick as a friend after our journey. He has returned the small support I provided him a thousandfold over the past few years.

***

EMP. The division of the anti-slavery forces seemed to take my father and our family down other roads. I know he grieved over the split and believed that it weakened our message to have diverse actions. While he had much respect for those who stepped over to the political side, he believed their efforts were futile, and I believe events bore him out on this count. At the same time, as we were smaller, this thrust my father forward on the national stage.

As he later makes note of, he became much more active in the broader AAS which, in turn, gave him access to a broader range of reformers. Through this activity, I believe, he was exposed to Parker and the other transcendentalists, Wendell Phillips, and others that he had not previously encountered primarily through trips to Boston and the East.

Of Frederick, my father always had the highest praise. As a man little acquainted with violence, he often told the stories of his time accompanying him, and he freely acknowledged the fear he felt in those travels. Frederick himself was a delightful visitor to our home as was most of the anti-slavery contingent. Polite to a fault, he exhibited the best manners of any man I ever encountered, including my beloved Burroughs. Likewise, he was a wondrous storyteller and could be counted on to regale those around him with tales of his days as a slave, his visit to England, or the experience of freedom in Nantucket. I count the time I spent with him as some of the best of my life.

On another note, my father makes frequent references to Abby, but they are mostly in passing. As a young woman she was my exemplar, my ideal. Of all I met in those years, I always believed she was the most intelligent, and the bravest. Facing down mobs, speaking alone on a stage, and converting the most hard-hearted to her words of wisdom, she personified all that was good about being a woman. If the abolition movement should split over the role of woman, I could think of no better example of why it should split than Abby.

Anti-Slavery

Truly, no man or woman was more worthy, and if any group was to drive her from their midst, they proved only their own intolerance.

I did not care for her husband's approach to reform as I found him too extreme, shouting out in the midst of various church services. However, she seemed to be happy with him although after her marriage we saw far less of her in western New York.

***

My involvement with Frederick and broader exposure to the movement cast me down another path—that of the famed Underground Railroad. Of that I shall make little note of here as our role was small. We, in Waterloo and Seneca Falls, were placed in such a way that we were a natural way station for those on the move from Syracuse to Rochester, or Buffalo, and hence to Canada. With people like the Posts and Frederick manning the western end, we housed the occasional escaped slave or family as they made the transit from Samuel May and others in Syracuse. Many of our Friends were likewise involved, and I never felt great risk in the endeavor. They were few and we were many.

Over the years I would guess that we harbored no more than twenty passengers in our home, and then only for brief times. I wagered that there was little risk of discovery, or fear of violence associated with this as almost all that we knew were likewise engaged, and even if the alarm were raised our passengers would be long gone. This turned out to be the case, and the only fear of violence I ever endured was associated with the escape of Jermain Lougen, and this was another matter altogether. My fear for the safety of my family was small, but I confess that I did carry a great disappointment for those that would wax eloquent about the rights of slaves yet refrain from assisting them when they were in need.

***

EMP. I think my father correctly assesses the family's role in this activity. While we all supported the assistance we provided as the right thing to do, we did not feel any undue alarm about our participation or fear of discovery. Our efforts were in no way like those who provided assistance in the states and cities that bordered the South.

I do remember waking on several occasions to find that we had acquired guests overnight. For the most part we provided what food we could, clothing as we had it, and, above all, a place to rest. For the most part, while we tried to engage those who were in our house in conversation, or provide amusements for the rare child, those who came through our doors were so exhausted and fearful that they had little inclination to expend needless energy in casual discourse.

***

As well, we joined with Frederick, the Posts, and others in 1842 to establish the Western New York Anti-Slavery Society. With the sad split of the movement in 1840, those of us who resided far from the centers of the movement believed that we needed to create a more cohesive body in order to move forward with our aims. The WNYASS was such a body, and while we were small in number, the organization did what we could organizing anti-slavery fairs to raise funds, supporting speakers in their travels, and continuing with our letter writing and petition campaigns.

Along with the Posts, we involved our efforts in encouraging Frederick to relocate to western New York, believing that a city such as Rochester would be more congenial for him. As we could, we provided funds to support his endeavors and portions of the monies raised from various fairs Lizzie and others organized went to his financial assistance as well.

With the aid of Garrison and others, I was also encouraged to become more active on the national stage. Accordingly, I served at

Anti-Slavery

various times on the Board of Managers of the Society and for a period of time as a vice president. The duties associated with these offices were not particularly arduous, although they did cause me to be away from Waterloo more frequently while in attendance at various association meetings or events. Fortunately for me, Elizabeth, with the assistance of Charles, was able to maintain the apothecary in my absence, and other than the heartache associated with missing my loved ones, it was not an undue burden.

Through theses exertions I found myself attending most of the major Meetings of the Society, and to my pleasure I became associated with the various luminaries of the cause that I had not yet met. While I found myself moving in broader circles, in truth, the movement seemed to lose a sense of progress. Yes, those such as Wendell Phillips stepped forward ably to carry the banner, but there seemed to be little end in sight. I do not believe the battle would have been won without the war, as there were many hard hearts that were not open to reason. I shall never know the truth of this, but I had become increasingly doubtful of our success.

***

EMP. As my father writes about various reforms, he seems to forget or dismiss other events that occurred during this time. Most notably he neglects to mention the death of Sarah. This was a tragedy for all concerned as we were all very close with her and Richard. They had made a loving marriage and produced three young children when she was carried away by exhaustion and the rigors of frequent childbirth. Other than Richard, my father and I took her death the hardest and his failure to mention her passing may be indicative of his feelings. It took all of us some time to erase her memory.

For Richard this was both a grievous time and a time of urgency as he needed to provide care for the young children at home. Accordingly Richard once again journeyed to Philadelphia to find a bride. While my sisters and I, along with a nurse, provided for the children, Richard ventured forth on a time-urgent mission. I should note that prior to this task he and my parents had identified prospective brides based on their knowledge of the Philadelphia Quakers. Among them was Jane Master, who Richard returned with shortly as his new wife. The small circle of our lives narrowed even more as Jane was the sister of Aunt Catherine, once again drawing us closer to the Trumans.

While I missed Sarah greatly, I grew to like Jane a great deal and we became close friends.

Chapter Eleven
Matters of Faith

While the coming women's convention caused much excitement and was well done, my own thoughts were elsewhere. Although the spheres were related as women's issues were a part of it, I was much occupied with the possibility of more discord among the Hicksite Friends.

Those of us at Junius had long advocated for the equality of the sexes in all matters of worship and had conducted both worship and business in that manner since 1838. Among the Hicksites we had kindred spirits, particularly in the Michigan Quarter and the Genesee Yearly Meeting. However, there was much wrangling over the issue of slavery and the Indians. More accurately, the discord was generated over the question of how active one should be in advocating for their views. We Quakers had long held to Fox's admonition to be "in the world, but not of the world," which most took as a constraint on activity in the political arena and the affairs of man. On the political side I had long held to this view and had not participated in the political process in any way other than to follow events in the public tabloids.

On the question of advocating for one's moral position, I disagreed with Fox. I had long held that mere words were insufficient if one truly believed them. Words required action and to not take action was a form of cowardice. This was consistent with my allegiance to Garrison and my actions on behalf of the slave. I did not believe one could consider himself a righteous man if he failed to take action. While I had long cherished the words of Fox, on this we parted ways. This, and other factors, led once again to my stepping off the cliff of dissent and putting feet to my faith.

While several years in coming, a number of us in the Genesee Yearly Meeting broke away in 1848 to form the Friends of Human Progress, later known as the Progressive Friends. We commenced with our first meeting, and from that meeting I, along with Rhoda DeGarmo, authored the Basis of Religious Association which I believe to be the truest testament of my beliefs and faith that I have espoused. Of all that I have written in my life, I am proudest of this document and have held to its tenets for the balance of my life. We created a Meeting that was open to the beliefs of all, free of the ranting of a clergy, and truly open to exploration of the human spirit. I was most gratified that our friends from Junius joined us in this endeavor. Indeed one could safely say that Junius became a Meeting of the Friends of Human Progress and was no longer Hicksite.

Once again I had cast my lot with a movement that ran the risk of costing me friends and associates, and to some extent it did. Certainly the move further estranged me from my old friends, the Orthodox, who I believe no longer consider me a Quaker. But among the Hicksite, while there was some repercussions, they were minimal. Indeed, almost all of my close friends and associates joined me in this endeavor which I found most satisfying. Even Lucretia, while never formally joining our ranks, shared our sentiments.

***

EMP. I certainly shared my father's sentiments in this matter, particularly given the actions that supported the rights of women as

Matters of Faith

coequals in all matters of faith. While I have moved away from the Quakers in matters of my own faith, I found the direction my father and mother took in this matter to be very congenial.

In reviewing this section of my father's manuscript and several others, another theme bears noting and that is my father's role as a leader. While true of my mother to a lesser extent, my father was a leader in many ways. Certainly in matters of faith he was recognized and acknowledged as a minister, but it went far beyond that. The power of his words, while simple and direct, moved others to action. He was compelling given both his words and his talent for living in a manner that was consistent with those words. Witness the way in which he had won over Waterloo, having been at one point a pariah for his anti-slavery views to becoming a respected and indeed venerated member of the community. One does not accomplish this through empty words and empty living.

Likewise, his range of leadership positions was impressive. At various times in his life he was a vice president of the Anti-Slavery Society, helped to found and lead the Western New York Anti-Slavery Society, served as Clerk of Junius and various Quarterly and Yearly Meetings, and was most definitely the leading figure among the Friends of Human Progress. As in all matters, my father would not have made this claim for himself, but I believe it to be true. One has only to look at the number of Friends from Junius who joined him in the Friends of Human Progress or those from Junius who put their signatures on the Declaration of Sentiments to ascertain the power he could exert if he but chose to.

As I have said several times, he was a reserved man in many ways and certainly not expressive, but he had a calm authority that attracted others. I have often thought that it was people like my mother and father, who labored without recognition or the desire for it, who truly ensured change in the way we live with one another.

Chapter Twelve
The Women

While our labors for the plight of the slave continued through the 1840s, a curious combination of events came together in Seneca Falls to raise another banner of reform: the rights of women.

In a household made up mostly of women, it was natural that much attention was paid to the injustice directed toward them, especially as so many women labored valiantly in the cause of the Negro. It required no great intellect, although many women of my acquaintance were great intellects, to realize that if one used the inalienable rights argument and applied it to slaves, then, by the very power of its logic, one must apply the same thinking to women. Frankly, I was much surprised that it took so long for the subject to rear its head, as it had long been a subject of discussion in Junius Meeting and among other progressive religious thinkers. Indeed, we in Junius had changed the discipline as early as 1838 to mandate equality among the men and women. In the broader sphere beyond the realm of reformers, however, little attention was paid to the issue.

In our home the rights of women were often compared to the rights of slaves and there was much vigorous discussion around the dinner table about the injustice of it all. All of the family, including Charlie, read the writers of the day who decried the injustices facing women and most could quote from Wollstonecraft, Grimke, Garrison, and others who penned remarks on the issue. While I did not reflect on it at the time, it was curious that the discussions did not lead to action until the arrival of Elizabeth Cady Stanton onto the scene. It has long been my hope that the women of my home felt that they were equally treated and thus were not moved by feelings of anger toward me to action, but I do not know this for sure. Mary Ann always reassured me on this matter, but I cannot gauge my true impact or my treatment of the women around me. I will leave that for my children and others to decide.

The summer of 1848 changed all that and transformed thought into deed. Much has been made of those days in July, primarily by Stanton but, to me, they seemed a part of a greater whole. Both Mary Ann and I had been much involved in the religious ferment occurring among the Hicksite Friends which was taking up much of our time and effort. As a large part of that debate centered on the rights of women and the anti-slavery cause within Meeting, the subsequent events of Seneca Falls seemed to be but a natural progression.

Of the convention and the events leading up to it, I shall say little as others have already started to write that history and have more passion for it. I do believe that the women ably acquitted themselves in both the organization of the convention and in the conducting of the actual meetings. This in itself was not a surprise to me, as all hands with the exception of Elizabeth Stanton had much experience with the organizing of fairs, meetings, and the like.

Instead, I was somewhat surprised that they would ask James and me to serve in the chair on the second day as most of the women had experience clerking meetings and other forms of public gatherings. I do know that they asked Lucretia to take on that task, but she demurred as she was not comfortable with the call for the enfranchisement of women and therefore did not feel she would do the meeting justice with both men and women present. To be clear,

The Women

I know that Lucretia was in much support of equality of women in all matters including the vote, but in this case she believed the move to vote was not timely and would distract others from the case as a whole. As in many things, her judgment on this was correct, as the call for the vote was really the only controversial part of the ultimate declaration. For myself, while I understood the passion around the franchise, it was of little note as I had chosen not to exercise it for myself.

Lucretia's fine hand was much in evidence throughout the entire process. Evidently she and Stanton had formed a bond while in London some years earlier and had made a pact at that time to hold a convention to discuss women's rights. It was Lucretia who brought Stanton together with Mary Ann and others at the Hunt house. Clearly as well, Lucretia would have understood that putting Stanton in front of a group of women who were committed to action would impel the entire group beyond rhetoric. It was often Lucretia's way to bring forces together that would create deeds that she supported, but not to directly tell others what they should do. Were she a politician, she would have been a superb one, juggling differences of opinion, building alliances, and nurturing the ideals of others.

The convention was, in my judgment, a great success and was attended by a goodly crowd of both men and women. Many fine speeches were given including ones by both Mary and Elizabeth that were, in my estimation, models of eloquence and truly inspiring for their parents, as it was a large public forum and the first time they had spoken both from their hearts, and in front of such a large promiscuous gathering. Of the declaration and the sentiments expressed, there was little true debate with the exception, as Lucretia had predicted, of the elective franchise for women. Had it not been for Frederick's strong endorsement of the right to vote and an impassioned speech on its behalf, I do not believe it would have carried the day, as many believed it would decrease the emphasis on other important concerns. But in the end it did as well as the entirety of the declaration.

For most in the audience, the days spent in the convention, the discussions that ensued, and most particularly the sentiments endorsed was time well spent. While we were small in numbers and existing in a western outpost, there was a sense that we had unchained great forces into the sphere of our civilization. My own role was small as I chaired the gathering during one session and made some remarks reflecting on Blackstone, but these were not of a substantive nature. The credit for the success of the convention justly lies with those who conceived of it and organized it.

I do remember that there was some consternation when it came to affixing one's name to the final declaration. While I and my family proudly placed our signatures on the document, as it was the right action to take in expression of our beliefs, there were others who either refrained at the time or later refused to affix their names. It was my understanding that many felt great pressure from business associates, husbands, or friends to disavow themselves from the proceedings and a number of otherwise good men and women suborned themselves to this pressure. In all more than half of those who attended the convention, participated in the discussions, and expressed their approval of the outcome failed to live out this support when it came to a more public form of expression.

After the convention, I, along with Lizzie, provided what support we could with a vigorous letter-writing campaign to the various newspapers and journals of the day. While Lizzie focused her attention on the anti-slavery periodicals, assuming we would find kindred spirits there, I engaged in writing the more prominent papers of the day, Greeley being the most notable. Like much else, our results were mixed. While many papers provided coverage of the convention, the results were discouraging. As we obtained the occasional enlightened supporter, just as often the men and women who participated in the convention had scorn heaped upon them.

It seemed, just as with our anti-slavery efforts, that the force of our moral arguments would not hold sway in the court of public opinion.

***

EMP. While my parents were in great accord with the rights of women, I know from later discussions with my father that he believed that retelling of the events of Seneca Falls lay with women, as he did not believe that the masculine view could present that tale with the fairness it deserved. Indeed, I believe he hoped that I would take up my pen in response, and I shall.

It was at Aunt Jane's house that the gauntlet was first thrown. While Mary and I had stopped in on that fateful day to pay our respects, we were not involved in the decision to call for the convention, although we were soon swept up in the excitement and planning. I believe, although I may have been introduced to her at some previous social event, that this was my first real encounter with Elizabeth Cady Stanton

My mother and the others at Aunt Jane's house were decisive women of action. To them words were empty without actions and accordingly they moved with great rapidity, quickly enlisting Mary and me in their efforts to bring about the convention. In this my father was also a great help as he was much respected by the members of Junius Meeting and had associations with the various local newspapers. Through him and with the assistance of Thomas Mumford, we placed announcements in the various newspapers and Mr. Mumford agreed to spread the word to other papers through his auspices. Fortunately we were able to obtain the use of Wesleyan Chapel for our purposes and the news of the convention spread rapidly among the area surrounding Waterloo and Seneca Falls. Likewise, we en-

gaged in a letter-writing campaign to our friends in Auburn and Rochester to enlist their support as well. In this we were successful and were able to gain the support of Frederick and the Posts from Rochester. Lucretia and my mother had much experience in organizing annual meetings and as a result the promotion of the convention proceeded with great dispatch.

Others have remarked with some surprise that we were successful in attracting a goodly crowd on such short notice. My view was just the opposite and I would have been surprised if we had not. Not only did we have the support of our stalwart friends at Junius and in the surrounding community, but we also had the appearance of Lucretia and Frederick, both of whom were guaranteed to gather a crowd wherever they spoke.

With plans under way for the convention, the second and perhaps more important task began to face us and that was to frame the discussion and agenda for the meeting itself. In this Mrs. Elizabeth Stanton was a great help. Almost immediately my mother and I invited her to our home to discuss the plans and she accepted, agreeing to meet with us on a Sunday afternoon several days prior to the convention. Accordingly, she met with my mother, Mary, and me to draft the sentiments for the meeting.

To use a phrase of the day, Mrs. Stanton came loaded for bear. She had clearly given much thought to the injustices facing women and came prepared with a list of grievances, legal issues, and complaints. In short order, I found much to like about Mrs. Stanton and discovered I was in much agreement with her views. She had a penetrating intelligence and was apparently well-read in law and other matters which stood her in great stead during our discussions. Personally I found her very congenial.

While passionate about her views, she combined her vehemence with good humor and warmth. While she knew not the first thing about organizing a meeting, she knew a great deal about the various

The Women

tribulations that women faced. In this I often wondered how much of her views were based on book learning and how much was based on personal experience, as she was busy with small children and her husband did not appear to support her efforts. Indeed, it was most noticeable that as soon as the announcement of the convention was made, Henry departed the area to work on political issues, not to be seen again until the convention was long over. While he was a vigorous champion of the rights of slaves, the matter of women and their rights seemed to escape him. Nevertheless it was clear to me from the outset that she and I would become friends and this indeed became true. For a period of several years we were very close and have maintained connections throughout the years, although not as intensely as we did in those first years in Waterloo.

About the drafting of the sentiments there is little to say. There was very little debate over the grievances that Mrs. Stanton had brought with her, although there was much discussion over her call for the franchise for women. Not that we disagreed with her view, but all were concerned about the practical implications of that viewpoint and how it might be received at the convention. On this our concerns were justified as it was the only true controversy at the convention.

Early on we agreed to use the words of Jefferson as our basis for our complaints, as their elegance was easily adaptable to our cause. In later years much was made of this, but I thought it was largely a fool's errand. I do not remember who first suggested that we use the words of the Declaration, but all supported it. I do remember that my father, when he dropped in on that day, was in great favor of it as he had much affinity for Jefferson's words and believed that they were at the core of the American soul.

In the end, although we struggled with some wording, we were all satisfied with the document and believed ourselves prepared to address the hoped for multitudes. In addition to the declaration, we made careful plans for the conduct of the meeting, the various roles that were needed, and identified a number of speakers on the topic.

I confess that I was almost overcome with excitement on the opening day of the convention. While we anticipated a good turnout based on comments from our friends, no one knew what to actually expect. As Mary and I greeted and seated those who arrived, we were thrilled with the throngs of women who streamed through the doors of the chapel. Attendance far exceeded what we had hoped for, and the attendance of numerous men was also most gratifying on the second day.

All went as we had planned. The declaration was read and discussed, numerous speeches were given, and the occasional word or phrase was changed in our original draft. But there was little discord with the exception of the call for the vote for women. On this matter, I believe the vote would have failed without an exceptional speech by Frederick aligning himself with both the rights of the slave and of women. The power of his words on this matter swayed the day and at the end of the convention our Declaration of Sentiments was carried much as we had originally written it.

My father makes note of the disruption caused by the signing of the declaration. On this I cannot comment as I faced no resistance, although I can certainly believe that this was true particularly for the men in the audience. As always I had no doubts that my father and mother would do what was right, and so they did.

I was most proud of my family throughout the convention. My father chaired portions of the convention with great grace, Mary gave an impressive little speech of her own writing and delivered it masterfully, and Sarah and Julia paid close attention throughout the proceedings. In the end, I was most proud to affix my name to the declaration along with my mother, father, and Mary. I felt as if I had been a part of something momentous and hoped that our efforts were not in vain. Little did I know the forces we had unleashed into

The Women

*the larger world, nor did I recognize the sentiments' pros and cons
we would dredge up.*

Chapter Thirteen
Aftermath

It has long seemed to me that the year 1848 marked a subtle change in our lives. In some way the pace of our days took on a new texture and substance, and in other ways our children began to move into the world as adults and independent vessels. It was a time of turmoil on all fronts—great passions were on the loose and others diminished. It was a time of love and tragedy, hope for a new day, and failure on other fronts. While there was great joy at many ends, there was also the constant reckoning with the baser instincts of man.

My greatest regret of the time was the travails that Lizzie was forced to undergo. If I could have taken on some of her burdens I would have, but the events that occurred were hers solely to endure. I have always been proud of my children, but for Elizabeth I held out the greatest hope. Perhaps as the eldest or because she always seemed to have a different direction, she held a different place in my heart.

From the time of our move to Waterloo, Elizabeth and I had spent many hours together in my store working alongside one another and conversing as well. It was clear as she entered into womanhood that she held a view of her future that none would hold as conventional. She was most adamant that she would someday strike out on her own into the world of commerce and make her way among men in that arena. On this matter, I was somewhat dubious as I knew of few women who had found success in this matter, but I tried to provide what support and encouragement I could.

Whatever the odds of success, I had no question about her abilities or capability in this area, as she consistently demonstrated her astuteness in trade. Indeed, I had became very much at ease with leaving the store in her care and under her direction. She was both good with our customers and exceptionally good with the keeping of our books; in fact, probably better than I, as it was not a task I enjoyed or felt proficient at.

Early on she had begun to explore opportunities in Philadelphia in several commerce houses, but delayed those ventures due to the needs of our business in Waterloo. After the convention, and perhaps inspired by that event, she reopened those explorations with my support and the encouragement of others. Little did I know the torrent that would unfetter.

While I had much experience with the deprecations of others and we had all seen the calumny expressed in the newspapers as a result of the convention, I was unprepared for the attacks she would undergo from men I had previously respected. I honored the right of others to hold different opinions from mine, and accepted that they would make different decisions as a result. I did not hold with personally attacking another for their views. That men would do this to my daughter I found detestable.

To put it briefly, Lizzie's efforts to obtain employment in Philadelphia were rebuffed with a noticeable lack of grace. Indeed, she was subjected to ridicule for her efforts by a number of men. Her response to all of this was exemplary. As she had spent time with Elizabeth Stanton countering the accusations foisted upon the convention, Lizzie and Elizabeth responded to the ridicule with satire of their own, publishing a short play that made a mockery of the

Aftermath

men and countering cartoons with their own drawn by Julia. In my estimation they routed the men on the field of intellect and fairness, but that did not result in employment for my daughter—only greater resolve to be successful in her own right.

Fortunately for all, Lizzie's frustration with those events was assuaged by the courtship of Burroughs Phillips. Phillips was the brother of the minister at Wesleyan Chapel and had come to Seneca Falls to establish a law practice. While not a Quaker, he was a fine man, and Mary Ann and I both approved of him. More importantly for us, so did Lizzie as we had feared she might live out her years without knowing the joys of marriage. Consequently and with some haste, she and Burroughs were married in 1852. It was a time of great joy for us, for just as Lizzie's courtship and wedding were proceeding, so was the courtship of Mary and James Truman.

***

EMP. I do appreciate my father's words of praise and companionship. Early on I determined that I would be beholden to no one and took the study of the ways of commerce quite seriously. My father and I had many frank conversations about this pursuit and he was clear, as he expresses, that he was a skeptic in these matters. Yet he was not skeptical about my abilities; on this he expressed no reservations but of the world and men in particular being able to exist as equals in commerce. Regardless, I was determined to proceed.

I should also say how much I enjoyed the hours I spent with my father as an equal. We had conversations about all manner of topics, and without fail he respected my opinion and right to have a point of view that was unique to me and different from his. The hours spent with him were akin to additional years of schooling as I learned much from him. While he could appear to others as fixated on the topics of religion and the slave, he maintained a wide range of interests and opinions.

The Memories of Thomas M'Clintock

As is my father's habit, he is brief about some things that matter most to me. Of the events regarding my potential employment in Philadelphia I could go on for pages, but I will not speak ill of the dead at great length. Suffice it to say that I was encouraged by my father and Lucretia to seek employment in the firm of her son-in-law based on favorable responses I had received to previous inquiries. I was greatly chagrined to learn that the men of firm did not support such an endeavor, and the flames of my anger were further fueled by the disparaging remarks of a few of those men.

My ire was further engaged through additional discussions with Mrs. Stanton, with whom I had grown very close. To say that she was outraged for me was to put it mildly. She gave me much support as we crafted responses, even going so far as to provide assistance in the writing of a short, satirical drama. I do not think my talents lie in literature, but I took great satisfaction in the lines we penned and the points we made in the debate. Likewise, we spent time together crafting responses to the various vitriol that was unleashed from the pulpit or in the newspapers of the day.

I confess to some confusion and ambivalent feelings about Mrs. Stanton's actions throughout these events. While we were great friends and shared many intimacies, I found her to be somewhat contradictory. On one hand she was quick to offer support and to incite action on the part of others, often crying in rage at the slights I had suffered. Yet, on the other hand she took little or no action that I could discern on slights that she had suffered at the hands of others—most notably her husband. She was, by turns, radical to the core in behalf of others, yet passive about her own existence. This became part of our falling out in later years.

Of Burroughs I can share much more. He was the love of my life, all that I wanted and could ever hope to have. While these words seem trite in hindsight, they are true for me. The brief years I spent with him and in his arms were the happiest I have ever been.

Aftermath

When I first laid eyes on him I was convinced he was the handsomest man I had ever seen; not that appearances were of great importance to me, but he was an impressive man. I was first introduced to him by his brother, Saron, at a social, and it was, for me, love at first sight. While I had scoffed at the romantic notions espoused in much of the literature of the day, his gaze and short conversation aroused great feeling within me. To later learn that he returned those feelings was a blessing. When I soon discovered that he possessed uncommon intelligence combined with great kindness, it was a gift beyond compare. Events moved rapidly and there was no doubt in my mind that I wished to spend my life with him. Consequently, when he proposed that we do so, there was no hesitancy on my part. Come what may, I wished to be with him even though I knew that choice would probably steal me away from my parents.

***

For the moment I will digress on James and Mary. Their budding romance gave me abundant pleasure. Given the frequent congress between George and I, James had decided to set up his dental practice in Waterloo around 1850—I forget exactly when—but he saw opportunity in the area. I know not if that opportunity included Mary at the time, but it soon came to pass as James quickly supplanted all other suitors. They had known one another for years, but there was no evidence of romance prior to James' relocation to Waterloo. This was quite fortuitous, as we not only gained a son, but he was able to treat my wife Mary Ann's frequent bouts of illness by removing her teeth.

Since the mid-1840s she had suffered a number of illnesses which seemed to leave her in a constant state of weaknesses due to her inability to eat much more than broth due to the pain that eating caused her. We despaired of remedy or treatment by a doctor, as we had long explored sundry other options. James and I debated various causes and cures, but in the end I agreed to his suggested course of treatment. For her part Mary Ann wanted only relief. To my immense surprise, James' treatment found success. While initially Mary Ann suffered discomfort as she adjusted to the teeth that James had hand crafted for her, she soon recovered. She remained healthy and as happy as ever from that day forward.

***

EMP. We had long worried about my mother's health. Years of rearing children and the labor associated with running a household had taken their toll. To be sure we all helped around the house with the sewing and other chores that felt endless, but my mother always seemed to do more or have more to do. At various times she suffered from excessive fatigue and we all worried constantly about cholera or the ague, so the relief she obtained from James' ministrations were a boon to us all. While I personally did not like the remedy and would not choose it for myself, it worked for my mother. How or why, I do not know.

My father liked James a great deal as did we all. While his travels and work took him and Mary away from us early on, I have much respect for his accomplishments. Both he and Mary were active at the Friends of Human Progress, Longwood, and under his care women were admitted to the dental school in Philadelphia. Even after Mary's untimely death in Germany, I have remained close to him. He has always been a stalwart friend and a fine man.

***

Besides George, James and I shared much in common. He was more than a mere dentist as he brought a chemist's perspective on all that he did. Indeed, he spent much of his free time exploring various properties for filling cavities and ultimately won some renown

Aftermath

for his efforts in this field. At the time it seemed that his experiment would lead to his death, as he suffered a serious explosion during the course of one such experiment which caused burns on his face. To this day, he wears a beard to hide the scars. Just as we mutually held an interest in chemistry, so we also engaged in common interests in progressive religion. For a man of science, James was exceedingly well-read on the subject, and he and I spent many an hour discussing in particular the merits of Parker's thoughts.

The early 1850s seemed to be the time of romance and marriage. While sincerely joyous for my children, I fretted about the impact these changes would have on our family. In short order, or so it seemed, Lizzie and Burroughs were wed, James and Mary Ann were married in our home, and Charlie found a bride as well. Only Julia and Sarah remained in our dwelling, which now seemed quite empty. The walls that once rung with laughter and mirth were quieter than before with the extended absences of the married children.

I spent much time thinking about what to do with my expanded family. James was well established in his own practice and lived close by, so that was not an issue. I had previously established Charlie in Seneca Falls under the auspice of Thomas M'Clintock and Son, and with his marriage, he and his wife, Lizzie, set up housekeeping in Seneca Falls. Elizabeth and Burroughs were something of another matter. Burroughs had no plans to permanently reside in our area, as the opportunities for a lawyer were somewhat limited. He made it clear from the beginning that he would return to the Syracuse area at some point in the future after his marriage. This announcement caused me some consternation. While I liked and respected all of my children's spouses, the family had never been apart from one another. Certainly I recognized that all children must spread their wings at some time, but it did cause me great heartache to contemplate the possibility. Not only did it seem that Elizabeth would depart, but the possibility of James returning to Philadelphia at some point grew real. Likewise, in my heart I did not believe Charlie was long for the life of a druggist. While he seemed content for the moment, I suspected he would also depart for other opportunities.

All this came to pass, but not in ways I had anticipated. Elizabeth and Burroughs did depart for Syracuse where they quickly established themselves, and Burroughs was on his way to being quite successful. He quickly gained the respect of many. With their move, Mary Ann and I began to consider our options as well, including moving ourselves to Syracuse. While we were now rooted in Waterloo and found it congenial, I longed for and missed my home in Philadelphia. As a consequence we discussed the option of moving to another location outside the Waterloo area.

But departure was deferred for some period of time and life continued in Waterloo with its small triumphs and struggles. In addition to the various romances of our children and the excitement that entailed, other events of note did occur.

***

EMP. Burroughs and I did depart from Waterloo for Syracuse, which was a torment for my parents. I was the first of the family to leave the nest, and this was painful for them. While they understood my need to do so, I think it reminded my father of his departure from his own family in Delaware and brought back unpleasant memories for him. He never said anything specific about this, but the pain in his eyes was evident.

Being in Syracuse did not imply that I was cut off from my family, as we exchanged frequent letters and visits, but it was not the same as before. Additionally, we had young Richard Hunt with us as a boarder, which maintained our connections to the family. While I was happy with Burroughs, I missed the daily congress and interchange with my father and mother.

Aftermath

Syracuse we found to be quite congenial and full of abolitionist spirit and like-minded souls such as Samuel May. We quickly moved into a routine of housekeeping, exploration of local events, and participation in the various movements that interested us. In many ways it was probably good for us to be away from my family as it allowed us the opportunity to settle into our own patterns and habits as man and wife. For many reasons it was the best time of my life.

***

Our family continued its effort to free the slaves, but the overall movement seemed to lag. Certainly I was more active within the AAS on the national stage and traveled more frequently in its behalf, but there appeared to be a curious lassitude among the members. For one, we were much smaller in number, which had its effect. Secondly, the various political machinations seemed to fragment the country and our movement. Those who espoused the political effort drained our efforts and national politics foretold of the coming secession movement. The resistance in the South hardened in support of slavery, and thoughts of changing their views through moral force diminished. The notion that the nation faced a choice between liberty and slavery was often articulated by prominent leaders on the national stage. All, combined with some personal factors, pointed to conflict and a fear of failure on our part.

The above, combined with some personal concerns which I hesitate to mention but will, took the wind out of our sails. The first of these plights was the loss of Frederick to our movement. I do not mean to infer that he no longer supported the abolition of slavery as he budged not an inch on that matter, but he chose to align himself with the political efforts and political parties rather than the force of moral suasion. Unfortunately, Garrison reacted very personally to Frederick's choice, which resulted in a great division between the two and much acrimony. This surely was a distraction to many, including myself as I believed Frederick to be our most prominent voice on behalf of the slave. While I remained true to Garrison and his principles, I mourned the loss as I cherished Frederick as a friend and champion of our cause.

The other personal factor was Garrison himself. While I hesitate to criticize him for all the good that he did, his voice became more strident and his positions grew more radical. William had long attacked the clergy for their passivity on the cause and cast arrows at the Constitution for its position on slavery. When he began to advocate for dissolution of the Union, I believe he chased away potential support for the slave. Certainly it was not any one position, but in every case William seemed to take the most extreme stance possible. He and I had several discussions about this, as I did not agree with all of his positions and believed some of them damaged our ability to gain support among the populace. While I supported his stance on non-violent means, his stance on women, and certainly his stance on slavery, in every instance he seemed to take the extreme view, thus pushing others away from us. Perhaps this is what saints do—they take the extreme point to force us to confront our demons and make hard choices, but in regard to practical considerations and the slave I believe those positions cost us support and consideration.

Lincoln famously said that a house divided cannot stand; that is what I believe happened with the anti-slavery movement. Our house had become divided and was less than it was before. Were it not for Stowe's book *Uncle Tom's Cabin* and the great, disastrous war, I do not believe slavery would have left our land.

In every quarter the potential for bloodshed as a means of resolution seemed to rear its head. When younger I had read Walker's *Appeal* from which I garnered some understanding of why the colored would or could resort to violence as a means to accomplish their ends, but I could not continence arms as a means for myself. I was dismayed with the events in Kansas and the tragedy of Harpers

Ferry. While many in the movement eulogized John Brown, I found his actions needless and abhorrent. I could not justify the slaughter of innocents in the name of any purpose and found the association of Frederick, Gerrit Smith, and Parker, all men I greatly respected, with that event to be a tragedy beyond reason.

In ways that I cannot fully explain, it appeared that we were winning the battle but losing that which was also important. As the 1850s progressed, more of the Northern population seemed to trickle over to the anti-slavery side. Stowe's book was a major factor in swaying opinion and slavery became a much discussed topic within the political arena. But for every step we took forward on that front we marched back two on the feelings toward our colored brethren. They were subject to all kinds of vilifications and deprecations that challenged their existence as human beings. Even the science of the day seemed bent on disproving the worth of the Negro. As was too often the case, I despaired for my fellow man and the narrowness of their thinking.

***

EMP. The recourse to violence, along with other events, seemed to crush much of my father's spirit. Gentle soul that he was, he appeared unable to accept the fact that those he knew and liked would align themselves with violent means. He withdrew into himself for a period of time. As always he returned, but his spirit reduced. Perhaps he was merely tired, but the violence and the continued threat of more violence seemed to dismay him and diminish him in some way.

Chapter Fourteen
Changes Among Us

As the abolition efforts intensified, my family and I did face some exposure to the reach of violence, although it was a distant brush. The infamous Fugitive Slave Act, allowing the recapture of escaped slaves, caused great consternation among many, including myself, and the events surrounding that act led to our encounter with the threat of violence.

Apparently events in Syracuse had transpired that led to an uprising of the citizens in the cause of a colored man who had been falsely accused of being an escaped slave. This, in turn, led the authorities in pursuit of Jermain Lougen, a colored minister, who had been a part of freeing the man. I had had some dealings with Lougen and Samuel May through my involvement in the Underground Railroad, and Lougen chose to flee to our home as he made his escape from Syracuse. While he spent but a brief night in our house, it was an evening of great tension as we did not know who was in pursuit, and when they might arrive. Lougen, heavily armed with weapons, spent the night watching for the signs of chase along with Charlie, but to out great fortune none arrived. To his credit Lougen asked my permission to carry his guns into our house knowing that it put us into danger should his pursuers arrive. While to my knowledge no gun had ever crossed our threshold, I granted his request although I feared the clash that might ensue.

Fortunately for all, the night passed without incident and Lougen departed at first light. He was a man of great stature in many ways, as evidenced by the kind note he sent us upon his safe arrival in Canada. I have followed his life from a distance for many years to find he went on to return to America and become a success. I take immense satisfaction in our small contribution to that outcome.

***

EMP. Somehow this event seemed to raise my father from his torpor and he returned to his old self, at least for a period of time. As always, taking action and acting on that which he knew to be right brought out the best in him. This night and the choices he made restored him, but in truth he was less than himself until after the war.

For me that eve was thrilling, although I recognized the possibility of danger. I passed much of the night with Charlie standing guard, and I do not believe anyone put their head to a pillow throughout the long, dark hours. Of all in the house, Lougen and my father remained the calmest and the two spent the bulk of the night in quiet conversation on the various occurrences in our country. Lougen was surpassingly courteous and serene throughout, even with the recognition of what might transpire and the risk he faced.

***

Progress on other fronts moved forward and provided much satisfaction. In particular, the Friends of Human Progress made impressive strides. As the title of our meeting changed variously over the years to Congregational Friends and ultimately Progressive Friends, I shall use the latter term to avoid confusion, as most have adopted it. We soon took on a meeting structure that was similar in many ways to the Quaker organization of Quarterly and Monthly

Meetings, with the difference being the equal influence of all and the noticeable lack of elders. I was honored for a number years through the appointment as one of the clerks of the Meeting. While this gave me no undue influence, it was a privilege nonetheless.

Likewise, the Meeting honored me with a minute to attend to the establishment of a Progressive Meeting at Longwood in Delaware. Mary and James had departed to Philadelphia and had been instrumental in establishing a free thinking group at Longwood. I journeyed there in the early 1850s to share what wisdom and help I could. I had been in and out of Philadelphia over the years on various trips involving my store supplies, the anti-slavery cause, or Hicksite activity, but this was the first time I had returned to the area of my ancestral home in more than forty years. It was a most gratifying journey. As always, I was able to visit my old and dear friends, the sessions at Longwood were successful, and I enjoyed a visit to my old homestead. Little remained from that time as the land had passed to others, but I could recognize various landmarks and with some effort was able to find and clear the family graveyard. I took some satisfaction in standing before the gravesites of my ancestors and speaking to them of my family.

***

EMP. As always, my father greatly underestimates his influence. In truth, I believe it was he who was the guiding force of the Progressives in Waterloo. Without his calm leadership, the Meeting would have failed and indeed it sank into obscurity after his departure from Waterloo. While James and Susan B. Anthony tried to maintain that which he had started, by the time of the war it was all but gone.

For a brief period it shone as a beacon of hope and I was an enthusiastic participant when I could be. The Meeting welcomed all and rang with vigorous liberal thought on all manner of topics. All the esteemed religious thinkers of the day were in attendance at various times and all opinions were welcome in an atmosphere of open discourse. It was the most stimulating Meeting and group of people I had ever encountered; all others have paled in comparison. For example, I know that my father took extreme pleasure in welcoming Parker and having him at the Yearly Meeting in the late 1850s. Despite my father's humility, he truly demonstrated the qualities and fervor of a natural leader.

***

For the moment I take pause to reflect back on what I have written, as it would appear that I judge my fellow man harshly and there is a part of me that asks, "Who am I to judge?" I have always claimed high hopes for what we can be. It has been my estimation that with proper toil mankind could create a heaven here on earth. There is much to hope for and strive for, and I always have believed that truth and goodness would prevail. In this I have found many like-minded souls—fellow travelers on the same journey—but there have certainly been others who have opposed those efforts with heart, soul, and fist. Those I find wanting and I do sit in judgment, however unfairly of them. They chose not to open themselves to the truth and they are less for it. I assume they will find forgiveness elsewhere when we will all be judged.

If this means that I am to be measured by my family as sanctimonious and dogmatic, then I accept that mantle however grudgingly.

***

EMP. As I read my father's manuscript, the above was included in the collection of papers dealing with the 1850s and I have placed it here as I believe he intended; however, it puzzles me. My father was the least judgmental person I know, at least in outward appearance. He greeted all as equals and maintained a cheerful countenance

Changes Among Us

with all he encountered regardless of their race, sex, or politics. I never knew him to be impolite to another or to make cruel comments about another, either to one's face or behind one's back.

Clearly, however, he was critical of himself and had moments of doubt and darkness that I was not privy to, much as we all are holders of secrets.

***

Before I close the chapter of my life in Waterloo, there are several other events to discuss. In many ways our life was very good, and the ten-year period between 1845 and 1855 was fruitful and harmonious. Mary Ann and I were happy together, our children were each successful in their own way, my business was on firm footing, and we had friends to cherish and who seemed to return that sentiment. It was a decade marked with the fruits of our labors and the blessings of God.

In addition to the events of the day which I have discussed previously, two events, one minor and the other a tragedy, served to mar our happiness. Of the first I shall say little, but note it as it had an effect on our children, and that was some discord with Elizabeth Stanton. She and Lizzie had been quite close for several years and worked together to great effect in the cause of women. Likewise, she had been involved with the Progressive Friends and participated fully in those Meetings. However, our Lizzie moved in other directions due both to her interest in commerce and her love for Burroughs, and this did not seem to sit well with Elizabeth Stanton.

As Lizzie became enthralled with Burroughs and naturally wished to spend time with him, Elizabeth Stanton did not take this diversion of interest with a courtesy. If anything, she seemed to grow more demanding—as I can think of no other word—of Lizzie's time and efforts. In the end, we all believed these demands to be unreasonable and as a consequence, we withdrew from Mrs. Stanton's orbit.

I have much respect for Mrs. Stanton and all that she has achieved over the years and her steadfastness in the women's rights cause, but I also believed her to be slightly imperious in her need for others to do her bidding.

***

EMP. I cared for and still care for Elizabeth. I hold the days we shared together in my heart. While our relationship is not what it once was, we have still stayed in touch over the years, and I have followed her advocacy for women with close attention.

While my father shares his perspective as a parent, I believe his assessment is accurate. Certainly my heart was moved in a direction away from the passions of Elizabeth, and when I would no longer do her bidding, I was shunted aside, soon to be replaced by Susan Anthony. Anthony has long filled that role and all credit should go to her as she has advanced the cause in her own way, and in ways I chose not to participate in. In the end, God worked the details out to the betterment of us all.

***

Of much more significance to my family and me was the death of Burroughs Phillips, the husband of Lizzie. By this time in my life I had experienced death in many forms, but Burroughs' death dealt all of us a blow we did not soon recover from, for reasons I cannot clearly deduce. Like all accidents that take a life, one is left to ponder the whims and capriciousness of fate and chance. Often in these cases we found ourselves plagued with more questions than answers as we struggle to find meaning out of the unknown.

Burroughs died from a head injury suffered in a carriage mishap. He lingered on for several days, but there was little that physicians could do as the extent of his injuries was beyond their capability. Fortunately I do not believe he suffered greatly, although he never regained consciousness and hence was unable to say good-bye to Elizabeth. For this reason I believe she suffered greatly. She had found much happiness with Burroughs relatively late in her life and to have that happiness stripped out from under her feet was grievous.

For a period of time following his death and her return home I feared for her health and sanity as she sank into a state of ill humor and exhaustion, barely communicating with anyone, seldom eating, and spending long hours alone in bed. Both Mary Ann and I worried about her and did what little we could to reassure her and comfort her, but all seemed for naught.

As a family we withdrew into ourselves, paying little heed to the day-to-day passing around us. Other than the needs of my trade or the requirement that we eat and maintain ourselves, we did little for several years in an effort to replenish and sustain Elizabeth. It was a dire blow for all of us, for we had learned to love Burroughs as a son and had much hope for his future.

In the end we all recovered and moved back into the world, but it required long, painful hours for all of us to get there.

***

EMP. Even from the distance of many years my father's words are a comfort. I do not know how to describe what occurred, for it is as if I went immediately from a state of bliss to one of utter desolation and anguish. All that I had, all that I hoped for, was dashed against the rocks of despondency almost overnight. My only blessing, and it was small, was that Burroughs did not suffer greatly, but I had longed to spend my days with him, to share his children, and to grow old alongside of him. And it was not to be.

My only thoughts were to return to the bosom of my family. Even there in the comfort of my home I was without consolation. My father writes accurately about this time as I retreated unto myself, along with my thoughts of hopelessness as I could see no light. I spent days, even weeks alone within myself with meager hope for the future, raging at the wrong that had been done to me.

My family was a great help through these months, although I feel that what I felt I passed on to them. It was a somber and dark household with little spoken but in quiet whispers, as if we might awaken the dead if we spoke as normal or, God forbid, gave any evidence of mirth.

How I survived I know not, yet at length I awoke as if from a lengthy slumber to return to the world of mankind. I roused myself from my bed, put off the clothes of mourning, and resolved that I must move forward. Oh, I rued in some ways that I had given my heart away to another and he had left me, but I resolved to hold his memory in a quiet place of my heart to visit when I needed the company.

I returned, but to where and to what purpose I was not sure.

***

The tragedy of Burroughs' death and our recovery seemed to galvanize us to action. While we had received much sustenance from our friends and the town folk, Waterloo no longer held the charm for us that it once did. As a family we began to explore other vistas and opportunities.

We were hastened on our way by Richard Hunt once again, although now for vastly different reasons. Richard had long been a quiet supporter of all that we did and certainly he was a benefactor to us all. Around 1855, however, he became suddenly very ill and even the careful nurture of George appeared to be of no avail in restoring him to health. He expired in 1856, soon after our departure from Waterloo. Even though we had long since passed the point of requiring his financial assistance, his impending death struck us all. We had no fears that Jane would change anything about the terms of our home or store, but we took his death, just as we did his courtship of Sarah, as an indication that our thoughts of moving were correct.

Accordingly, as a family we made plans to depart from Waterloo almost twenty years after we had first arrived.

Chapter Fifteen
Home to Philadelphia

Where to go was initially an unresolved question, although we all wanted to be closer to Philadelphia; given Mary Ann and my advancing age, we desired somewhere to the south where the winters were milder. Both Mary Ann and I suffered bouts of rheumatism and felt the cold of the Waterloo winters most acutely.

After some exploration, we resolved to move to Easton, a short train ride from Philadelphia. I had concerns about my trade given the rise of professional schools, and as Charlie did not care for the life of a druggist, Easton offered us the chance to move in a new direction in the making of vinegar. While there seemed to be no immediate Meetings that were in sympathy with our views, we resolved to make the move nonetheless. We were able to obtain housing that was most pleasant and find a place for the production of our product, and so we departed. We would leave behind James and Mary Ann, but even then it was clear they would be returning to Philadelphia in the near future.

Times had changed, and our good-byes and the move were easier in many ways. I was able to sell my stores at a good profit and consequently there was less to pack and ship. Where once we had made the long, slow trip by canal to Waterloo, now everything traveled by rail, which made both the shipping of our goods and the trip itself far simpler and faster. All in all, the move was a simple process. Likewise, where once we had traveled with small children, now all were grown and able to fend for themselves, which was an enormous relief, except for those like Charlie who were bringing their own children. To onlookers we must have looked like a wagon train heading West as we packed multiple families and headed off to the East.

Saying good-bye was not as difficult as it had been when we left Philadelphia. While we had made many friends in Waterloo and Seneca Falls, bidding farewell to them was not as painful as our departure from Philadelphia, as we did not have the same emotional ties that we did to those in our old home. Somehow making friends with others as an adult proved different for me than those I had known since I was a young man. As well, we looked forward to a return to friends, so we were not venturing into the unknown. I confess that I received some small satisfaction that the same community where once I had been hung in effigy now encouraged me to remain with my family. Their entreaties were most pleasant to my ear, but their pleas were too late as we had resolved to leave and once again start anew.

Even with twenty years there, Waterloo was never our permanent home, and there were few tears shed on the part of Mary Ann or myself.

***

EMP. I will say little about our departure or Waterloo. For myself, I wanted to be somewhere else that was beyond memory of Burroughs. Every street and landmark in Waterloo carried vivid memories which I wished to bury and leave behind. I was also resolved to venture into commerce, and I knew that the Waterloo area was not the place for me to engage in that endeavor. As well, those that were closest to me were joining me in the venture to a new town.

***

About our years in Easton I have little to mention, as in the scheme of things it was but a brief moment. Our time there was pleasant, but without much in the way of event or turmoil, which was perhaps what we all needed at the time. It was a respite for us and, in some ways, a further retreat from the trials of the world. We left no mark there, nor did we feel the need to do so.

Very quickly, or so it seemed, we pulled up stakes from Easton and returned to my beloved Philadelphia. The impetus for this move occurred on multiple fronts. The vinegar business I did not find much satisfaction in and neither did Charlie. After years of attending to the needs of customers, the task of manufacturing vinegar I found to be boring and tedious.

For myself, I was aware that I needed to return to my trade and Philadelphia offered the most opportunity as I was already known there. Charlie as well found little to like in the vinegar trade. He seemed to enjoy the buying and selling associated with it, but like me, he did not enjoy the process of making vinegar. In truth, I worried about his future as it did not appear that he had landed on anything that engaged his fancy. As events would play out, his experience in buying and selling was his true calling, as he discovered after the war.

While this process and learning was unfolding, James and Mary had removed themselves to Philadelphia both for opportunity, and for the fact that George had suffered some ill health. James very much wished to be closer to him in his latter years.

The push to go came from an unexpected source—Elizabeth. Unbeknownst to either Mary Ann or me, Lizzie had explored the opportunities in commerce in Philadelphia, found a store to rent, and had made a decision to open her own trimmings establishment in Philadelphia. Clearly she was going with or without us, as when we first heard of the possibility it was already an accomplished fact. As she had her own funds from ventures she had made into the salt business, it was her decision to make the great leap into the world of commerce.

It took little encouragement for us to pack our bags and join Elizabeth on the flight to Philadelphia. At long last, I was going home. I could not pack fast enough, as I was afraid that should I blink, the chance would disappear.

***

EMP. My father presents a very evenhanded review of this matter, although I do not remember it quite the same way. Make no mistake, my parents were always supportive of my pursuit of a life in commerce, and my father had offered me funds, just as he did with Charlie, to establish myself, although I never made use of that offer. I remember my parents as being quite upset about the whole matter. In the main, however, I think their reaction had little to do with my business venture and everything to do with my failure to discuss the idea with them in advance. In this they are probably correct, although I was well past thirty at the time and had my own funds to use. Notwithstanding their concerns, I had done all that my father indicates, and by the time I discussed it with them, the transaction was complete. No matter what they might have said, there was no turning back.

I am not sure why I took the tack I did with my parents, for generally I had discussed all matters with them prior to making a decision. In this case, I believe it served as a small test for me that I could do all this on my own, recognizing that if I was to be successful there were choices and decisions I would have to be solely accountable for in the future. I was fortunate as well that some small

Home to Philadelphia

monies that Burroughs had left me and the results of a venture into salt mines was sufficient to provide me with the capital I needed to begin in the world of commerce. I have never regretted the choice that I made and it has served my purposes for many years.

***

We returned to Philadelphia not in triumph having vanquished our foes, but quietly as was our wont pouring into the arms of our friends and greeting all as long lost comrades. We set up housekeeping with all of the family surrounding us, each going about their own business, but returning at night to the confines of familial comfort and mutual love.

For myself, I returned to the trade I had long known and set up a small apothecary shop that was sufficient for our needs. I no longer supported a vast brood, and Mary Ann and I were able to do with far less than when we were raising a family of seven. Additionally, each of the children pitched as they were able and I no longer knew the long hours and toil I once had. It was a grand comfort to me as my bones told me that I could not continue to work with the vigor that I had in my youth. Each of our children was soon successful in their own manner with even Julia and Sarah finding employment that provided satisfaction for them.

As usually followed, we were soon swept up in the events of the day and found like-minded Progressive Friends with whom to associate. It was a great joy for me to be reunited in friendship with George and Abraham. While each of us could visualize the end, we reconnected with the bonds of more than fifty years time.

***

EMP. Our return to Philadelphia marked the return of smiles to my father's aged face. Our latter years in Waterloo had been marred by much death, and I realize now how affected he was by that when

I recollect that he did not seem to smile for years! Philadelphia brought the sparkle back into his eyes and his joy was manifestly evident for all to see. He reveled in delight to be back among his friends.

For myself, everything my father wrote earlier when establishing his own emporium held true for me. I was vastly fortunate to have Sarah by my side as my assistant, but even then there did not seem to be enough hours in the day. My parents were of much support to us through the initial years of business, as our success was delayed to some degree by the outbreak of the war. In the end, however, I take much satisfaction in all that we were able to achieve.

***

All else seemed to be subsumed with the impending election and the threat of succession by the Southern states. While I chose as always to refrain from the vote, I was much caught up in the outcome. I had heard Lincoln speak on one occasion in Philadelphia and I was duly impressed with him. He spoke almost as a Quaker would with few gestures, and his eloquence was direct and to the point. Early on I placed my hopes on him due to his expressions of anti-slavery sentiment, but I was appalled at the venom that was unleashed by the Democrats in his direction. Constantly did they play the race card and impugn Lincoln with all manner of vile and disgusting words. To his credit he did not respond in kind, but deflected the barbs hurled at him with patience and good humor.

My erstwhile support of Lincoln was not popular with my abolitionist associates, for they took him as a typical politician out only for himself. In the end my support and faith in him was justified, but there were numerous trials and many months before that justification was reached. After his election I was initially disappointed with his lack of action on the slave question, although in hindsight I

Home to Philadelphia

recognize that he may have had larger issues to deal with given the rapid dissolution of the union and subsequent war.

With Lincoln's election, the terrible war followed. I cannot vouch for its justification as I was and always have been opposed to war and violence as a means of resolving the affairs of man. In my heart I cannot deny my satisfaction with the outcome and the consequent elimination of slavery, but it is difficult to reconcile that outcome with the terrible cost. Thousands of lives lost, untold destruction, and millions of dollars thrown away was a horrible price to pay. I rejoice in Lincoln's emancipation of the slaves, but I shudder and mourn the loss of those who sacrificed their lives, no matter the worth of the cause.

We, like our neighbors and friends, followed most of the war through the newspapers, searching for new insights and scanning the casualty list for those we knew. All were touched by the reach of the battle, and we were not immune to its call. Early on Charlie made clear that he felt he must answer the call. For a Quaker such as myself and given all I supported in my life, this discussion placed me on the horns of dilemma. On the one I supported the peace testimony of my brethren and had little truck with war. On the other I saw the Union campaign as a way to erase slavery as an institution from our shores. Truly it was not my choice but Charlie's and he, like many of our Quaker friends, stepped forward on the Union side. I admired that he would make a choice of his own free will rather than taking the easy way out and hiring another in his stead.

While I do not know the specifics, I would hazard a guess that half of the Quaker families I knew likewise sent sons to war bearing arms. While I have long struggled with the question and given my age never had to face it, I suspect I too would have made the choice that Charlie did if the circumstances were the same.

So Charlie went to war and we remained behind in fear for him. To the best of my knowledge he served in an honorable fashion and was promoted to the rank of major by the end of the war, although according to him he saw little action. But that did not allay our fears on a daily basis. Like all parents during the conflict, we waited for word of new battles and carefully tracked where our sons' units were in relation to those battles. We went to far too many funerals and memorial services during those years not to be realistic about what could occur to our son as well. Fortunately for all, he came through combat unscathed and returned home more self-assured and mature than before. We breathed a mighty sigh of relief at the war's end. Our joy was tempered only by the tragic assassination of Lincoln.

***

EMP. My parents worried constantly during the time Charlie was away. As their only son, rightly or wrongly they placed great hopes in him. While his return was a matter of great joy for them, both seemed to have been aged by the war. While each of them lived on for a number of years after the War, they now seemed old and withered. The war took a toll on all.

***

The war seemed to mark the end of many things. We discovered that the bonds of nationhood were hard won. The loss of life on both sides left long-standing wounds, and the American Anti-Slavery Society ceased to exist through the will of Garrison and the agreement of the members. There was some debate on this matter, as many looked forward to a new day and the chance to work with the former slaves on their transition to citizenship. Countless Quakers took this step after the war, but it was the will of the Society that its work was done. We would go forward as a footnote to history overshadowed by the war and the Emancipation Proclamation. It would be for others to determine if a lifetime effort would be acknowledged or even remembered.

Home to Philadelphia

We did hold one last hurrah in the city where the movement had started, meeting in Philadelphia for last time in 1864. It was a bittersweet event. Many had known one another for thirty-plus years and we had seen one another through countless sorrows and successes. Not only had we worked together in a common cause, but we had shared deep bonds of friendship. We had opened up our homes, exchanged news of children and birth, and intimately integrated our lives with one another. While no one said it explicitly, there was a sense that many of us would never see one another again. Either death would claim us, as for the most part we had aged together, or circumstances would not bring us together; it was a time of many speeches of celebration, copious weeping by all parties, and much grief.

In a time of victory over the ills of slavery, there was a great sadness as well. Many of those in attendance I never saw again and I remember them all with great fondness and respect. I did correspond with many and continue to do so, but the common bond that held us together had been broken.

***

EMP. My father captures the mood of the meeting accurately as I was there. While much younger than most, there were those I wished to greet as well. In particular I wished to meet with Abby and convey my thanks to her, which I did. She had remained youthful in appearance and maintained her enthusiasm for reform, although she was accompanied by her husband whom I had always thought too extreme.

In the main it was a somber affair with more evident sadness than satisfaction in a job accomplished. While many would move on to other reforms and other action, for others in attendance it was if their lifeblood had been drained from them, and I suspect many felt a void in their hearts for all they had labored for.

The Memories of Thomas M'Clintock

For my father, he seems to harbor questions as to the legacy of the movement. As with many causes, he seems to doubt if there was achievement, if their efforts had borne fruit. In my mind there is no question. The men and women who made up the anti-slavery movement, who stood fast in the face of great odds, were the shapers of our destiny, a reminder of who we were as a people. They consistently demonstrated that an individual could do what is right for another with little or no hope of reward simply because it was the just and Christian thing to do. Each and every one of them, no matter what the contribution, deserves our praise and accolades. They were warriors in the silent battle for truth, and that alone is a great victory.

***

My life has run the course of the small stream, turning this way and that, but constant in its direction to join with the greater body. My remaining days cannot be many, but I rejoice in what I have.

Through the grace of my children, and particularly Elizabeth, Mary Ann and I have been able to retire, or at least that is what they call it. We are able to remain close by to our children and also spend time in Vineland, which we find to be remarkably congruent with our beliefs. I have returned to my pen and have written numerous pieces that echo themes I discussed forty years prior. It is reassuring to know that I can still think and present logical thought.

Elizabeth is successful and better in the world of commerce than I have ever been during all my years as a druggist. She and Sarah do well together. Julia has found a niche as a teacher of art within a Quaker school, which proves a fine application of her skills. Mary Ann and James remain happy together, although his work takes him to distant Germany. He and Mary are altogether too busy, their life marred only by the death of their two young daughters, but their son, Howard, survives. Only Charlie seems to have permanently departed, heading out with family to the oil fields of Pennsylvania. We see them far less often than I would like.

As for me, I am with Mary Ann and that is all I ever really wanted. We have celebrated fifty years of marriage to one another with our friends George and Catherine, Lucretia and others. During those fifty years I do not think we ever said a cross word to one another, which is undoubtedly a tribute to Mary Ann's patient nature, and not me.

I look across the room at the woman I have loved for more than fifty years and she always remains the young girl of twenty that I married. We can still read and often hold one another's hand while doing so. I can think of nowhere else I would rather be.

Epilogue

EMP. My father's closing words I will let stand, as they were written and are below. I can do him no greater honor. It is my sincere hope that I have lived up to his words in my own life.

Of our family I would say a little to account for all. My parents have both passed on and are joined with one another at Fair Hill. Theirs was a true union of more than fifty years and a joy to behold. My sister, Mary, passed away in distant Germany and lies beside her parents. James returned with their surviving son Howard and has gone on to an admirable career in Philadelphia. Charlie became Charles, or the Major, as a result of his experience in the Civil War and lives in Oil City with his wife and children. He survives. Julia and Sarah reside together with me. We split our time between our work and the community in Vineland, which has provided us with much abundance. Only our Heavenly Father knows what awaits us in the days beyond.

***

Of late I have been engaged in correspondence with my grandson, Howard, regarding a number of issues, including his upcoming visit to Waterloo and the great falls at Niagara. As is my wont as a grandfather, I have been warning him of the dangers of the falls and admonishing him to take care when visiting. In turn, he has been regaling me with his latest reading interest. He informs me that he has been following the adventures of a family named Peterkins, about whom a series of stories have been written. Apparently, as Howard tells it, the family is completely lacking in anything remotely resembling common sense. And this is the gist of the stories—how someone helps them out of their troubles by prescribing a common-sense solution. His interest in the topic mystifies me, but apparently he finds reading the stories a source of great mirth.

His stories do, however, provide me with a theme. I have surpassed my allotted three score and ten and I am aware that most of my life is behind me. From my vantage point it has been a life well spent.

For my part, I end with questions remaining in order to sit in judgment of myself. I have become convinced over the years that what religion one holds is of little consequence. That is not to say that religion is not of value. Indeed, I believe it is of the greatest value, and how one settles oneself in relation to God is a critical question. There is much to be said in the Bible and other writings that is both worthy of note and guidance. But which religion one holds to or one's exact beliefs about God are of no matter in the grander scheme of things. For it is how one acts that is, at the end of the day, the issue for all of us. Jesus' exposition of the golden rule is the guide we should all follow. How we treat our fellow man is the ultimate lodestone.

But life's judgment falls on more than that; for if I chose to treat my fellow man, my neighbors, and friends well, and turn a blind eye to the injustice that surrounds me in the world, I have failed and become less human. Less than I could have been if I had applied myself. God exists in all of us and if I ignore that spark of divinity in

Epilogue

each of us, I fail. It was this understanding that led many to treat others as less than human when in fact our equality is God-breathed.

And so I believe the greatest good is seeking out injustice, intolerance, and ignorance and forthrightly challenging those errors, those misstatements of the truth. To do less than that for any of us is to fail in the eyes of God. By this standard, I believe I have tried to the best of my ability. Often falling short of my own hopes, I have striven to right wrongs wherever I have chanced upon them. Upon that I will accept what judgment may come.

And therein lies common sense, as each of us must determine what is true and where our path lies for ourselves.

I close with hopes for the future as the days must be brighter than the ones we recently passed through. I close with hopes for my offspring, that they will retain justice in their vision going forward. And, I close with the three words I have long used to say good-bye and good wishes to others.

Blessings attend thee.

Selected Bibliography

I deliberately chose not to footnote this book and to write it as fiction. For those who desire to do additional reading on the topic, I have included some suggestions as well as the known writings of Thomas M'Clintock.

Abzug, Robert. *Cosmos Crumbling: American Reform and the Religious Imagination.* 1994. New York. Oxford University Press.

Barbour, Hugh et al (eds) *Quaker Crosscurrrents: Three Hundred Years of Friends in the New York Yearly Meetings.* 1995. Syracuse. Syracuse University Press.

Bacon, Margaret. *Mothers of Feminism: The Story of Quaker Women in America.* 1986. Philadelphia. Friends General Conference.

Bacon, Margaret. *Valiant Friend: The Life of Lucretia Mott.* 1980. New York. Walker and Company.

Bordwich, Fergus. *Bound for Canaan: The Underground Railroad and the War for the Soul of America.* 2005. New York. Harper Collins.

Brown, Slater. *The Heyday of Spiritualism* 1972. New York. Pocket Books.

Collins, Gail. *American Women: 400 Years of Dolls, Drudges, Helpmates and Heroines.* 2003. New York. Harper Collins.

Commager, Henry S. *Theodore Parker.* 1936. Boston. Little, Brown and Company.

Cross, Whitney R. *The Burned-Over District: The Social and Intellectual History of Enthusiastic Religion in Western New York, 1800–1850.* 1950. New York. Harper and Row.

Dorsey, Bruce. *Reforming Men and Women: Gender in the Antebellum City.* 2002. Ithaca. Cornell University Press.

Douglass, Frederick. *Life and Times of Frederick Douglass: His Early Life as a Slave, His Escape from Bondage and His History Complete.* 1995. Secacus. Carol Publishing Group.

Dubois, Ellen C. *Feminism and Suffrage: The Emergence of an Independent Women's Movement in America.* 1848-1869. 1999. Ithaca. Cornell University Press.

Fox, George. *The Journal.* Penguin Books. 1998. New York.

Ginzberg, Lori D. *Elizabeth Cady Stanton: An American Life.* 2009. New York. Hill and Wang.

Selected Bibliography

Goodman, Paul. Of *One Blood: Abolitionism and the Origins of Racial Equality*. 1998. Berkley. University of California Press.

Griffith, Elisabeth. *In Her Own Right. The Life of Elizabeth Cady Stanton*. 1984. New York. Oxford University Press.

Harrold, Stanley. *American Abolitionists*. 2001. New York. Pearson Educational.

Hawkes, Andrea Constantine. *The Life of Elizabeth M'Clintock Phillips, 1821-1896: a Story of Family, Friends, Community, and a Self-Made Woman.* Thesis (Ph.D.) University of Maine, 2005 Unpublished.

Hicks, Elias. *Journal of the Life and Religious Labours of Elias Hicks*. 1832. New York. Isaac T. Hopper.

Hinks, Peter P. *To Awaken My Afflicted Brethren: David Walker and the Problem of Antebellum Slave Resistance*. 1997. University Park. The Pennsylvania State University Press.

Ingle, Larry. *Quakers in Conflict: The Hicksite Reformation*. 1998. Knoxville. Pendle Hill Publications.

Jeffrey, Julie R. *The Great Silent Army of Abolitionism: Ordinary Women in the Antislavery Movement*. 1998. Chapel Hill. University of North Carolina Press.

Lynd, Staughton. *Intellectual Origins of American Radicalism*. 1969. New York. Vintage Books.

May, Samuel J. *Some Recollections of the Antislavery Conflict.* 1869. Boston. Mnemosyne Publishing.

Mayer, Henry. *All on Fire: William Lloyd Garrison and the Abolition of Slavery.* 1998. New York. St Martin's Press.

McPherson, James M. *The Struggle for Equality.* 1964. Princeton. Princeton University Press.

Morgan, Edmund. *American Slavery, American Freedom.* 1975. New York, WW Norton.

Newman, Richard. *Freedom's Prophet: Bishop Richard Allen, the AME Church and the Black Founding Fathers.* 2009. New York. NYU Press.

Quarles, Benjamin. *Black Abolitionists.* 1969. New York. Oxford University Press.

Palmer, Beverly W. (Ed). *Selected Letters of Lucretia Coffin Mott.* 2002. Urbana. University of Illinois Press.

Penney, Sherry H. and Livingston, James. *A Very Dangerous Woman: Martha Writhgt and Women's Rights.* 2004 Boston University of Massachusetts Press.

Perry, Mark. *Lift Up Thy Voice: The Gimke Family's Journey from Slaveholders to Civil Rights Leaders.* 2001.New York. Penguin Putnam.

Selected Bibliography

Perry, Lewis and Fellman, Michael (Eds) *Antislavery Reconsidered: New Perspectives on the Abolitionists*. 1979 Baton Rouge. Louisiana State University Press.

Reynolds, David S. *John Brown Abolitionist: The Man Who Killed Slavery, Sparked the Civil War and Seeded Civil Rights*. 2005. New York. Alfred A. Knopf.

Sernett, Milton C. *North Star Country: Upstate New York and the Crusade for African American Freedom*. 2002. Syracuse. Syracuse University Press.

Sklar, Kathryn K. and Stewart, James B. (Eds). *Women's Rights and Transatlantic Antislavery in the Era of Emancipation*. 2007. New Haven. Yale University Press.

Stamp, Kenneth M. *The Peculiar Institution: Slavery in the Ante-Bellum South*.1989. New York. Vintage Books.

Stanton, Elizabeth Cady. *Eighty Years & More: Reminiscences 1815-1897.* 1993. Boston. Northeastern University Press.

Stauffer, John. *The Black Hearts of men: Radical Abolitionists and the Transformation of Race*. 2001. Cambridge. Harvard University Press.

Stebbins, Giles. *Upwards of Seventy Years*. 1890. New York. John W. Lovell Company.

Stewart, James B. *Holy Warriors: The Abolitionists and American Slavery*. 1997. New York. Hill and Wang.

Stowe, Harriet B. *Uncle Tom's Cabin*. 1852.

Tolles, Frederick (ed). *Slavery and the Women Question: Lucretia Mott's Diary of Her Visit to Great Britain to Attend the World's Anti-Slavery Convention of 1840*. Supplement No. 23 to Journal of the Friends' Historical Society. 1952.

Walters, Ronald G. *American Reformers 1815–1860*. 1978, 1997. New York. Hill and Wang.

Wellman, Judith. *The Road to Seneca Falls: Elizabeth Cady Stanton and the First Woman's Rights Convention*. 2004. University of Illinois Press.

Winch, Julie. *A Gentleman of Color: The Life of James Forten*. 2002. New York. Oxford University Press.

Wollstonecraft, Mary. *A Vindication of the Rights of Woman*. Penguin Books edition.

Yellin, Jean F. and Van Horne, John C. (eds). *The Abolitionist Sisterhood: Women's Political Culture in Antebellum American*. 1994. Ithaca. Cornell University Press.

Thomas M'Clintock's Writings

Publications

"Essays on the Observance of the Sabbath." Philadelphia, Joseph Rakstraw, 1822.

Selected Bibliography

"New York Yearly Meeting," *The Friend: or Advocate of Truth*, 1 (July 1828).

"Observations on the Articles Published in the Episcopal Recorder, over the Signature of a member of the Society of Friends." New York: Isaac Hopper, 1837.

"Extract form a private letter dated, Waterloo 5th month 28, 1839," *Pennsylvania Freeman*, 14 June 1838.

"Henry Clay and the Society of Friends," *Pennsylvania Freeman*, 2 May 1839.

"Thomas M'Clintock Letter," *Liberator*, 12 September 1839.

"Mr. Garrison – His Past Course and Present Position," *Liberator*, 27 September 1839.

"Thomas M'Clintock," *National Anti-Slavery Standard*, 16 July 1840.

"Letter from T. M'Clintock to the Association of Friends for Promoting the Abolition of Slavery." 1840.

"To the 'Association of Friends for advocating the cause of the cause of the slave, and improving the condition of the Free People of Color," *National Anti-Slavery Standard*, 16 July 1840.

"Basis of Religious Association," 1848.

(with Rhoda DeGarmo) "An Address to Friends of Genesee Yearly Meeting, and Elsewhere," in *Proceedings of the Yearly Meeting of Congregational Friends, held at Waterloo, NY* (Auburn, NY: Oliphant's Press, 1849).

Letter from Thomas M'Clintock" in *Proceedings of the Yearly Meeting of the Friends of Human Progress held the 7th, 8th and 9th of June, 1857, at Junius Meeting House. Waterloo, Seneca County, NY* (Rochester, NY: Curtis, Butts and Co., 1857).

"The Irrepressible Conflict," *National Anti-Slavery Standard,* 15 December 1860.

"Letter to a Member of Congress," *National Anti-Slavery Standard,* 27 December, 1862.

"Principles and Peculiarities of the Society of Friends," *The Friend* 1 (September 1866) (November, 1866) (October, 1866) (July, 1866).

 "Letter from Thomas M'Clintock," *The Friend,* August 1866.

With J.G. Whittier "A Letter," *The Friend,* September 1866.

"Letter to a Clergyman," *The Friend,* May 1867.

"Second Letter to a Clergyman," *The Friend,* July 1867.

"The Christ Doctrine, and Views of Paul and his Fellow-Believers Regarding It," *The Friend,* September 1867.

"Examination of the Terms Used by Paul in Teaching of the Christ-Doctrine," *The Friend,* October 1867.

Selected Bibliography

"Son of God, Christ and His Body, etc.," *The Friend,* November 1867.

"The Law and the Gospel," *The Friend,* April 1868.

"The Late Conventions," *Index,* 17 December 1870.

"Is Christianity Absolute Religion?" *Index,* 11 June 1870.

"The Modern Principles," *Index,* 4 February 1871.

"A.W.S and the Catholic Father," *Index,* 1 May 1874.

Letters

FHL = Friends Historical Library, Swarthmore College
SHGP = Sydney Howard Gay Papers
AKFP = Abby Kelley Foster Papers

To Elias Hicks, 5 October 1821, Hicks Papers, FHL

To William Poole, 19 November 1822, Burr Manuscripts, FHL

To William Poole, 2 April 1823, Burr Manuscripts, FHL

To William Poole, 22 December 1823, Burr Manuscripts, FHL

To Elias Hicks, 1 January 1825, Hicks Papers, FHL

To Elias Hicks, 10 January 1825, Hicks Papers, FHL

To Elias Hicks, 1 April 1825, Hicks Papers, FHL

The Memories of Thomas M'Clintock

To Elias Hicks, 1 April 1828, Hicks Papers, FHL

To William Poole, 6/ 9 June 1825, Burr Manuscripts, FHL

To Abby Kelley, 10 January 1843, AKFP

To Sydney Howard Gay, 4 July 1845, SHGP

To William Logan Fisher, 20 July 1849, Historical Society of Pennsylvania

To Sydney Howard Gay, 23 August 1848, SHGP

Acknowledgments

This is a work of fiction and has been a labor of love, as I hope it is obvious to the reader that I have great affection for both the M'Clintocks and the times in which they lived. As my historian friends remind me, the one thing we can never know about history is what people were truly thinking during various events. As a consequence, any opinions or thoughts that I put into the mouths of Thomas or Elizabeth are solely my interpretation of what they might have thought or felt. Likewise, any errors of historical fact are mine alone. While I have tried to reflect the historical record as accurately as possible, there may be errors, others may have different interpretations, or new data may come to light. On the latter issue, I certainly hope so, as more research will only contribute to our knowledge of the truth.

Writing this book has been a journey along which I have encountered numerous helpful people, some of whom don't know it as I used their research or books at various points but had no direct contact with them. I'd like to thank them at the risk of offending those I have left out.

First and foremost are my wife, Debra Dinnocenzo, and my daughter, Jennimarie. They have read every word of various drafts of this manuscript and offered their comments, encouragement, and editing—including vigorous debates on the proper use of commas. More importantly, they have provided constant support and encouragement including numerous trips to Seneca Falls, allowing me the time to complete this book, and constant love. This book would have been far less than it is without them.

At various stages of the book I have had others read drafts and provide feedback. As I suspect with most authors, it is a nerve-racking experience to open your words up to the scrutiny of others, and I am indebted to them. Among those who have offered comments are: various cousins and friends, and in particular Mary Beth Neely, Kathy Shomo, Tom Smith, Maria Smith, Shirley Mayton, Kathleen Voss, Reid Smucker, Vivien Rose and Chris Densmore. While the words in the book are ultimately mine, their comments and critiques have made it far better than it was originally.

Pamela Guerrieri of Proofed To Perfection graciously served as the editor on this book. She was a joy to work with. Her comments, suggestions, and compassionate approach made this work far, far better than it was originally.

There are numerous authors whose work I have drawn upon for this book. I have included a bibliography but wanted to mention several authors who were particularly significant. These include: Judith Wellman, Andrea Hawkes, Ronald Walter, Richard Newman, Larry Ingles, and Christopher Densmore.

Last but certainly no means least—in fact, they are probably the most important group to me—are the various historians, curators, National Park personnel, and other M'Clintock "fans" that I encountered over the years. They have been unfailingly gracious with their time, interest, and willingness to respond to my often obscure or uninformed questions. It's a long list but they deserve the praise:

- ➜ The people of Seneca Falls and Waterloo. Without fail I have been met with warmth and kindness by the people of

Acknowledgments

Waterloo and Seneca Falls. Their hospitality has made the area a home-away-from-home for my family.
- → The staff at the Women's Rights Historical Park. In particular I want to thank Jack Shay (retired), Anne Derousie, and David Malone. They have been unfailingly kind to my family and me and, in all ways, represent what is best about the National Park Service. It's a rare treat to go to one of our nation's national parks and be greeted by name.
- → Christopher Densmore, Curator of the Friends Historical Library at Swarthmore College. Chris has been incredibly generous with his time, interest, and expertise throughout this process. He is the best representative of the Society of Friends that I know—constantly and in many ways demonstrating his concern for others and humanity. He is forever uncovering small nuggets of information on the M'Clintocks and unfailingly shares those insights with others. His review of my manuscript and helpful comments on Quaker practices was invaluable. He is also the only person I know who has an original of Hicks' *Peaceable Kingdom* in his office.
- → Vivien Rose, Curator at the Women's Rights Historical Park. Like Chris, Vivien read and commented on a draft of this manuscript from her perspective as an expert on the events of Seneca Falls. She went out of her way to take on this task and my appreciation for her assistance knows no bounds.
- → Andrea Hawkes. Andrea's dissertation on Elizabeth M'Clintock Phillips is the treasure trove of information on the M'Clintocks. Meticulously researched and lovingly written, I hope she is able to turn her dissertation into a book. Her subject deserves to see the light of day.
- → Judith Wellman. *The Road to Seneca Falls* is the definitive work on the events of the Women's Rights Convention of

1848. For anyone who is interested in the early women's rights movement, it is well worth the time to read it.
- Historic Fair Hill Burial Ground. The Quakers in Philadelphia have done a superb job of both restoring this National Historic Site and involving the local community. They have created a small oasis in the midst of Philadelphia that honors the Motts, Trumans, M'Clintcocks, Purvises, and other reformers who are interred there.

Historic Locations/Web sites

There are numerous sites and locations still in existence which play a role in this book or are sources of additional exploration for the reader. Obviously, Philadelphia is one of those locations and is worth delving into in its own right, not just because of the M'Clintocks. Several other locations also merit your visit. Among these are:

- The **Women's Rights Historical Park** (www.nps.gov/wori/index.htm) in Seneca Falls, NY. The Park contains the restored home of Thomas and Mary Ann M'Clintock as well as the home of Richard and Jane Hunt, the Stanton home, and the remnants of Wesleyan Chapel where the original convention was held.
- **Friends Historical Library** (www.swarthmore.edu) at Swarthmore College, Swarthmore, PA. The library holds the letters of Thomas M'Clintock and a vast collection on the Society of Friends.
- **Longwood Progressive Meeting** in Delaware.
- **The Smithsonian Institution** in Washington DC. The M'Clintocks' original parlor table on which the Declaration of Sentiments was drafted is the property of the Smithsonian.

- **Fair Hill Burial Ground** (www.fairhillburial.org) in Philadelphia. The M'Clintock family, with the exception of Charles, is interred at Fair Hill, which is a National Historic Site. It is fitting that the M'Clintocks are buried there with their friends George and Catherine Truman, James and Lucretia Mott, and numerous other reform-minded Quakers.
- **Photographs:** While some photographs of key individuals are included in this book, others are not due to space. Should you want to see additional pictures of the participants, the best source is the Friends Historical Library and the online collection of the Truman-Underhill Albums. This collection contains pictures of the Hunts, Trumans, M'Clintocks, Motts, etc. You can reach the site by entering http://www.swarthmore.edu/fhl.xml and searching for the Truman Underhill collection. Additionally, photographs of many of the abolitionists (Garrision, Douglass, and Thomas M'Clintock) are included in the collection of the Massachusetts Historical Society.

About the Author

Rick Swegan has spent the bulk of his professional career as a consultant and sales person in human resources. He is currently a senior consultant with a major human resource consulting firm.

Personally, he is the proud descendant of both the M'Clintocks and the Trumans, and has spent the last ten years researching and studying his family, the movements they were involved with, and the times in which they lived. Previously he co-authored with his wife, Debra Dinnocenzo, the book *Dot Calm: The Search for Sanity in a Wired World*.

Rick speaks frequently on the topic of the early women's rights movements, is a member of the Friends Historical Association, and has taught on the subject of the early Women's Rights movement at the Chautauqua Institution.

He resides in Pittsburgh, PA, with his wife and daughter, while spending as much time as he can in Chautauqua, NY.

More information on Rick is available on his Web site, www.rickswegan.com or at Facebook at *The Memories of Thomas M'Clintock*. You can reach him via e-mail at rick@rickswegan.com or engage in discussion with him via Facebook.

The Memories of Thomas M'Clintock

Rick donates a portion of all the proceeds from this book to the Women's Rights Historical Park in Seneca Falls, NY.